The city was a jungle of geometries

Barrabas loped along the graveled roof, then jumped down to the neighboring rooftop, scrambling over giant pipes and dodging the huge exhaust installation from a ground-floor restaurant. He searched for his target, his finger leaning on the trigger.

Switzer stood in the open behind the chimney. He swung around, bullets belching from the fiery muzzle of his rifle. Suddenly Deke Howard appeared from nowhere, holding his pistol in a two-handed grip. He jumped to the top of the chimney, blasting as he went.

Switzer yelped as blood blossomed along his arm from elbow to wrist. The rifle jumped from his hands, skittering across the asphalt and stopping at Barrabas's feet.

The assassin stepped sideways, clutching his mangled forearm. "Back off!" he bawled desperately. Then his eyes cleared, and he was trying to laugh.

"Just back right off, boys," he sneered, edging closer to the door of the stairwell. "'Cause we got your girlfriend, Barrabas. Anything happens to me—she's history, man. She's dead!"

SOBs
SOLDIERS OF BARRABAS

SOBs
SOLDIERS OF BARRABAS

NO SAFE PLACE

JACK HILD

A GOLD EAGLE BOOK FROM
W🌐RLDWIDE

TORONTO · NEW YORK · LONDON · PARIS
AMSTERDAM · STOCKHOLM · HAMBURG
ATHENS · MILAN · TOKYO · SYDNEY

First edition November 1987

ISBN 0-373-61621-X

Special thanks and acknowledgment to
Robin Hardy for his contribution to this work.

Printed in Canada

1

It was November, and it rained. The Atlantic drizzle bled the grayness from Manhattan's stone canyons, diffusing it up and down long wet avenues, wrapping the upper stories of the skyscrapers in misty gauze. The streets were slick, shiny as black mirrors. The thinning leaves on the trees around Madison Square, green thinning to autumn yellow, seemed to be the only vestiges of color remaining in the soggy city.

Fifth Avenue and Broadway had been closed to traffic. The intersection where the two famous thoroughfares crossed was almost deserted except for a handful of soldiers dressed in camouflage fatigues. Military vehicles, jeeps, four by fours, ambulance trucks and loden-green sedans were parked along the curb on Fifth Avenue and around the statue of a long-dead general. Officials, some in civilian clothes, others in dress uniform, waited under umbrellas on a small reviewing stand at the edge of the park.

A yellow light glowed bravely through the drizzle from the top of a flagpole. In New York, this ersatz electric fire was known as the Eternal Flame. Fifth Avenue ran like a river between the stone bluffs of high buildings on either side. Several blocks away, the first banners carried by solemn marchers emerged from the mist and the drizzle. It was a holiday, but even in a city of fourteen million people, few came to watch a Veterans Day parade in the endless rain. A tall, powerfully built man stood in a doorway on Fifth Avenue, the collar of his trench coat pulled tightly around his neck, his hands in his pockets. A small torrent of water suddenly poured from an overloaded eavestrough overhead, spattering his crew-cut, nearly white hair and dripping onto his shoulder. He stepped farther back, pressing himself against a store window, and wondered why the only witnesses to the living and the dead of America's wars were the great edifices that ringed the square, shoulder to stone-cold shoulder.

It wasn't as if the weather was too much of a hardship. He had lived for days in rain that made this look like spit, with nothing to eat and little more than rags on his back, in hostile and forbidding lands, where detection meant torture and death of the most hideous kind. He never thought himself a hero for it. Nor had any of the other men marching down Fifth Avenue. They had been soldiers. It went with the job.

It seemed like such a small thing to ask, for people to come out on a rainy day to remember those who had fought for America's freedoms, and those who had died. But at Madison Square, the only spectators were the police who manned the blue barricade across Fifth Avenue, and the odd passerby who momentarily slowed on the way to shelter in the nearby subway station. And the rain.

With little fanfare, the first marchers approached through the steady drizzle, a ragged line of men in raincoats, bearing umbrellas and American flags and a purple banner declaring a Jewish veterans' organization in bold yellow letters. But their shoulders were back, chins forward, and they walked proudly, oblivious to the stormy weather. They came to a stop on the far side of the flagpole in orderly columns. Other marchers poured into Madison Square.

There were regiments of soldiers and sailors, young servicemen in uniform from nearby bases who cast curious sideways glances at Manhattan's gray and unfamiliar sights, a marching Coast Guard band, their ceremonial hats carefully shielded from the rain by plastic wraps. There was a dwindling group of white-haired old men, some wearing leg wrappings, their chests bespangled with medals proudly won in the First World War. A larger group of middle-aged men had mixed civilian clothes with ill-fitting Second World War uniforms. Several dozen Asians passed in careful formation, their green banner, almost as wide as the street, declaring the U.S. Korean Veterans' Group.

But by far, most of the marchers had shared the war that marked the silent spectator in the trench coat. Carrying banners from Brooklyn, Queens, Westchester, Connecticut, Long Island, they were no longer the young men they had once been, the naive and the innocent, American teenagers hauled off to fight a crazy Asian war for a political principle that had been abandoned after fifty thousand of their friends were already dead. Some were bearded, others had long hair, many now bore paunches. All had one thing in common: they had survived Vietnam. They filed into the square, several hundred of them, lining up beside the young men in uniform, filing slowly forward past the reviewing stand to place their flowered wreaths at the foot of the flagpole.

The mayor of New York entered the square on foot, surrounded by dignitaries and aides. He mounted the reviewing platform, eschewing an umbrella, and stood hatless and solemn in the cold, unrelenting rain. A late-model station wagon, painted camouflage green, slowly entered the square. Carefully anchored to the roof was a bamboo cage.

The man with the crew cut shivered. Memories didn't return. He refused to allow them. But the feelings never left. A pair of boots hung from a bamboo strut, and an iron chain was coiled around the framework of the tiny prison. Two men paraded in front of the car, their banner black, the white-lettered message short and to the point: RELEASE POW/MIA IN SE ASIA.

By now, a small line of spectators had gathered despite the soggy weather. Suddenly there was a commotion on Fifth Avenue. People with video cameras and notepads left the shelter of parked cars and vans. They rushed toward a group of several dozen marchers who paraded behind a large white banner bearing an inverted pink triangle. Flashbulbs popped. Heads turned among the soldiers and veterans who stood in orderly columns in the square. The marchers stepped bravely forward, with only the slightest hint of doubt or uncertainty in their eyes. The words on their banner were blocked by the horde of photographers and journalists jockeying for a better shot. A woman in a yellow raincoat ran with a microphone, jabbing it at the faces of the men who carried the banner, assaulting them with questions.

The silent observer in the trench coat stepped forward for a better look, oblivious to the drizzle, when suddenly he felt movement to his right. He turned sharply, his instincts honed from more than twenty years of perpetual warfare. A short man with the girth of a cement truck pushed against the window and stood beside him.

"This is the first year they let that veterans' group into the parade," Walker Jessup drawled, the accent of his native Texas unmistakable. "'Course, they came armed with a court order this time."

The marchers passed by the two men, their eyes set nervously straight ahead, journalists trailing after them like a pack of hungry pariah dogs. Their banner was clearly visible now. GVA. Gay Veterans' Association.

"Only in America," Nile Barrabas murmured, his eyes following the marchers as they entered the square. A small smile of amusement came to his face. The marchers stopped, keeping a slight distance from the columns of veterans and soliders already in position.

"I knew this was going to make trouble," Jessup sighed.

Barrabas nodded slowly, then shook his head and glanced at the sky with wry humor. "Sure is a gloomy day, but it seems to suit the occasion."

The fat man bobbed his head, the layers of chin quivering against his neck. "Uh-huh, here come the brass with their speeches. You know the old saying—talk is cheap.''

Several dozen officials, with the exception of the hardy mayor, cowered under umbrellas on the reviewing stand. A man stood to introduce the speakers. The rain had put the sound system out of order, and he was forced to shout over the heads of the assembled veterans.

Barrabas turned away from the street and looked at his friend. "What are you doing here?"

"Same thing as you, I imagine. Just paying respect to a few old buddies I can't see around anymore. Anyone in the crowd you know?"

Barrabas almost shook his head, but stopped himself. "Sure. All of them. In a way. Doesn't matter if I know their names and faces when we've all been through the same thing."

Jessup eyed him balefully, and finally nodded, understanding what the soldier meant. "You heading off to the Caribbean today? The schedule you filed with the agency..."

"Little change of plans. Thought I'd stay in New York a little longer."

The burly Texan looked surprised. "What's her name?" He winked.

Barrabas smiled again but resisted an answer. Goddamn Jessup was psychic. He got his nickname, "the Fixer," because of his talent for arranging covert operations on a private basis to the highest bidder—usually an agency of the U.S. government. Nile Barrabas was his chief operative, the leader of a group of highly skilled commandos who styled themselves the Soldiers of Barrabas, the SOBs. But the mercenary's private time was private. If the Fixer was really interested, he could find out on his own.

On the reviewing platform, the mayor had just finished his speech and was introducing the next speaker. An umbrella separated itself from the others. A general, rows of colored braid lining the pockets of his massive chest, moved to the front with the lumbering gait of a prowling carnivore. Barrabas stiffened. This year's parade's star attraction. The man he had come to see. General Hieronymous Guetz.

"Blood and Guts." It was the nickname Jessup had learned for the general fifteen years ago when he arrived on his first rotation as a CIA officer in Saigon. "That's how we got to know each other. In 1974 when he assigned us both to—"

"By my time he was just known as General Blood," Barrabas interrupted. His words were cold and emotionless. The tall man's face had whitened, and his lips were set in a rigid grimace.

Jessup stared at the warrior's face for a moment, surprised. Something between revulsion and contempt was written there. The mission up the Kap Long River to infiltrate Chan Minh Chung's headquarters and steal the Vietcong battle plans had been successful. Walker Jessup had ridden aboard a patrol boat, the *Callisto*, to pick up the survivors behind enemy lines. There was only one. Barrabas.

A VC ambush at some narrows in the river had almost stopped them. A bullet had pierced Barrabas's helmet, peeling the metal back and penetrating his skull. It stopped fractions of an inch from his brain.

A week later, when he regained consciousness in a Saigon military hospital, Barrabas's dark chestnut hair had turned almost entirely white. Jessup had debriefed him on the mission, but the bullet also appeared to have left a partial amnesia. Barrabas had come through with the battle plans, but could recall little else.

Something had happened on the Kap Long River that had changed Nile Barrabas forever, and it was more than just a matter of physical appearance. That had been almost two decades ago. But the expression written across the war hero's face on this rainy morning was hard and real. Jessup shivered and turned away. He knew Barrabas sometimes walked close to the edge. He'd hate to see the man lose control.

"Hey, c'mon, Nile," he coaxed gently. "Let's grab some breakfast—" Suddenly a shout broke from the ranks of veterans. A tall, exceptionally lean man in camouflage fatigues and aviator sunglasses had grabbed the banner with the pink triangle from the hands of a marcher. Shouting epithets, he began to rip the fabric down the middle.

Reporters ran forward, once again jostling for position. City police jumped from the barricades. A tall blond woman who stood among the gay veterans leapt toward the attacker and pushed him away. He raised his arms, sweeping her hands aside. The men who had been carrying the banner retrieved it from the wet pavement and valiantly tried to raise it. On the sidelines, Walker Jessup blinked twice to be sure.

"That's—"

"Deke Howard," Barrabas finished, striding across the sidewalk toward the fracas.

The police waded through the crowd while news photographers contented themselves with snapping pictures. Veterans and soldiers and the rear of the columns turned to look at the commotion. The officers and officials at the reviewing stand, some distance away, appeared oblivious to the commotion. General Guetz cleared his throat and withdrew a sheaf of papers from his pocket. His voice boomed over the assembly.

"My fellow Americans..."

Deke Howard grabbed the banner again, ripping it halfway down the middle when the men who held it resisted. "Ya fuckin' sickies!" he shouted hoarsely. He tugged the banner again. It ripped more. Rather than see it destroyed, the men who carried it let go. Howard threw it onto the rain-slicked street and stomped on it. The men who had marched behind the pink triangle surged forward to protect their banner.

"Fucking perverts." Howard leapt into the air and landed, feet apart, hands stretched in a karate position just as several police officers arrived at the center of the fray. He turned slowly, his hands stiff and winding in small circles in the air. The gay veterans backed off. The police moved forward, and Deke kicked at them, forcing them to back away.

"Lieutenant Howard! 17th Waterborne Assault Group, 'tenshun!"

The order was stiff with unforgiving authority, the voice of someone who was accustomed to being obeyed. Deke Howard froze, his eyes searching the crowd that had gathered around him in a wary circle. Suddenly there was a gap in the crowd, and the tall man with crew-cut white hair stepped into the center, his face rigid with wrath. Howard gasped. He jumped to attention. Nile Barrabas stood, tall and forbidding, his blue eyes narrowed as he stared at the unruly man. The police started to move in on Deke Howard. Nile Barrabas put his arm up. They stopped. The mercenary stepped forward until he was inches away from Howard's face.

"Lieutenant Howard, are you a soldier or a coward?"

"A soldier. Sir!"

"And do you salute your commanding officers or not?"

"Yes, sir!" Howard snapped out a salute.

"Yes what?"

"Yes, sir, Colonel Barrabas!"

The mercenary leaned in closer and whispered. "Deke, I'm going to kick your ass good for this." He knelt on the rain-soaked street and lifted the dirty banner. Turning to the men and women who had marched behind it, he handed it over.

"I apologize on behalf of this soldier."

The vets took it, their faces filled with a mixture of curiosity and gratitude. The sonorous tones of the general's speech floated across the square as if nothing had happened.

"I'll take care of this man," Barrabas snapped at the police, gripping Deke Howard by the lapel of his camouflage jacket.

"I thought this was for soldiers, not for a bunch of—"

"Shut up, Deke."

Barrabas hustled him to the sidelines through an opening in the crowd. He stopped when they reached the bronze statue of the general.

"Colonel, I didn't fight a war for America for that... They ain't no comrades of mine," Howard protested sullenly.

"Haven't seen you, Deke, since the day you piloted the *Callisto* down the Kap Long River," said Walker Jessup, slipping beside the two men.

Deke Howard put his hands into his pockets. He rocked from foot to foot, looking down at the sidewalk.

"Howdy, Jessup. Colonel Barrabas, it's great to see you again," he said in a low voice, casting tentative embarrassed looks at the two men. "Been a long time." He gestured with a nod of his head back toward the crowd. "It just don't seem right..."

"Be like a man, and you can ignore it even if you don't like it," Barrabas told him.

"It didn't seem to make any difference in Nam," Jessup concluded with wistful seriousness.

"So how you doing, Deke?" Barrabas socked him lightly on the shoulder and smiled. The veteran looked at the mercenary, his admiration evident.

"Doin' great, Colonel, Walker! Civilian for the last ten years. Just started working for the general!" Howard beamed and pointed toward General Guetz. The retired officer remained at the front of the podium across the street, reading from the soggy sheets of paper he held.

Barrabas's reaction was almost imperceptible, but the Fixer was highly skilled at noticing subtle reactions. The colonel had flinched. For Jessup, it was a first. Kap Long, he thought. The ghosts of Vietnam. But anyone who had been there was one of two things: haunted or dead.

"You okay now?" Barrabas demanded.

Howard shuffled his feet nervously. His face was gaunt, with lines etched deeply at the corners of his eyes. "Sure I am. But I still don't like it," he said, his lip curling.

"Deke, there are a lot of things we don't like that we have to live with." Barrabas extended his hand. "It's good to see you again."

The men shook hands, and Deke disappeared back into the crowd.

The general's speech came to its conclusion, his words carrying clearly across Madison Square. "We have learned the lesson of Vietnam!" he cried. "War cannot be fought in half measures. To defend democracy, we must go all the way—"

"I thought the lesson of Vietnam was no more war, period," Jessup muttered.

"Blood and Guts always talked that way," Barrabas said stiffly. "Breakfast?" He nudged Jessup.

The Fixer's eyes lit up. "The very suggestion is sustenance." He slapped his massive stomach and smiled eagerly.

The two men started walking, and the gray drizzle fell without cessation.

2

Jessup sat in the plush high-backed swivel chair, leaning his elbows on the polished surface of his long black granite desk. The view behind the sixty-fourth-floor plate glass window of his midtown Manhattan office was one of impenetrable white. The top of the skyscraper was completely enveloped in cloud. Occasionally it was possible to detect slight movement in the nebulous vapors beyond the glass, when a strong Atlantic wind batted against the side of the building.

From November to March, New York was awful, shades of gray upon gray. And business was slow. Vacation, he thought. The idea warmed him. Bermuda. It sounded so appealing. And there was a restaurant there, run by Cuban exiles he'd once helped by extracting some of their relatives from a Havana prison. He was always welcome there. He snapped his fingers. That was it. The cure for the pre-Christmas blues.

He fumbled with a key in the lock of the bottom left-hand drawer and withdrew a foot-high stack of papers sheathed in cardboard covers. Walker Jessup prided himself on having the most extensive collection of menus from the finest restaurants in the world. Certain of their archival importance, he had bequeathed them to the Metropolitan Museum in his will. For the time being, however, they were merely useful. He found the one he was looking for, an over-size folder with a red-velveteen cover. The restaurant was called La Guanillo. He opened the menu, and his eyes feasted down the long list of entrées and appetizers, consuming lists of desserts and cheeses. Salivating madly, his stomach churning with desire, he turned to the wines.

For twenty years, Walker "the Fixer" Jessup had been one of the top operatives for "the Company"—as the CIA was affectionately called by its employees. Little more than a quarter of the way through his career, he'd stopped counting the number of times he'd cheated death. After three wrecked marriages and two decades of clandestine service capped by four years in Saigon, enough was enough. He retired and set himself up as a private consultant in international intrigue with a little black book of names and telephone numbers that intelligence agencies the world over coveted. Always a big man, and with little desire for another masochistic attempt at wedded bliss, Jessup surrendered to the inevitable. He got fat.

Me and Marlon Brando, he mused, patting his enormous belly. His weight had dropped to two-ninety. He could afford a vacation. A real pig-out. Bring it on! he demanded of no one in particular, slamming the menu shut and shoving the pile back in the bottom drawer. Cholesterol! Sodium! Red meat and white sugar! Carbohydrates for days!

He aimed his index finger toward the button on the office intercom, all set to make reservations, when something occurred to him. Money. He didn't have any. Damn, he thought, snapping his fingers in anger. It was a bull market on Wall Street, and he'd climbed aboard for ten days, plowing everything but reserve funds for his consulting business into his investment portfolio. And business had been slow. Cash flow was a problem.

The dream of La Guanillo began to fade when the intercom buzzed obnoxiously, abruptly interrupting his gastronomical reveries.

"We have a client, sir!" Ducett, whom Jessup had taken on as a personal assistant after the young man's four-year stint in the Airborne, sounded excited.

Jessup froze, his index finger suspended in midair. A client. He could use one. He looked longingly toward the bottom left-hand drawer, palpably aware of the odor of La Guanillo's chocolate chicken permeating the room. It was amazing what his imagination could do to his olfactory nerves. Food, client. Client, food. The debate raged.

The intercom buzzed impatiently.

"Mr. Jessup? Sir? It's General Hieronymous Guetz. Retired, that is. Sir?" Ducett prodded urgently, but more with awe than emergency. He whispered in clearly audible tones, "The famous war hero, sir!"

Originally a farm boy from Georgia, Hieronymous Guetz had started to rise to prominence when he'd become a war hero in Korea. Fame was assured when he led American troops in the invasion of Cambodia in the early 1970s. By the latter days of the war, he was responsible for the operational theater in the provinces of Saigon.

He turned into a figure of controversy when he advocated a policy of total war, and his units bragged of the consistently highest body counts. When reports of a bloody civilian massacre surfaced in the home press, General Guetz narrowly escaped being directly implicated. Quietly discredited, he had been forced into a low-profile desk job at the Pentagon by the next White House administration. A few months later he retired and disappeared from the public eye. Recently, with the current administration's preoccupation with Central America, he had risen to prominence again, riding the speech makers' circuit to round up support for a hard line. It was a sign of his return to the public eye that he had been invited to address the Veterans Day rally at Madison Square.

The Fixer hesitated again but only slightly. What in hell did Blood and Guts want with him? he wondered. But he knew the answer. He knew what all his clients wanted before they even opened their mouths. Tricky business. Risky business. Dirty business. They came to the expert.

Jessup knew which side his bread was buttered on. It was a pay-as-you-go business. A client meant a fee, a fee meant food. But for the time being, farewell, Bermuda! La Guanillo, adieu! Jessup's index finger landed on the Talk button.

"Send him in!"

General Guetz entered Jessup's office in a boisterous, comradely manner. He was a big, barrel-chested man with a thick, craggy face. Even at the age of sixty, he maintained a youthful vigor. His hair was dark brown, whitened only a little at the edges of his side-burns.

The Fixer rose to greet him.

"Long time no see, Walker!" the general boomed jovially, shaking Jessup's hand tightly with his right and slapping him hard on the shoulder with his left.

The Fixer winced, motioning to a chrome-and-leather chair. He squeezed his enormous bulk back into the swivel chair behind the black granite desk, flexing his hand and rubbing his shoulder.

"I think it was on an aircraft carrier in the South China Sea," Jessup said, smiling tentatively. "At the very end of it all."

"Or the very beginning," Guetz piped up, leaning back in the chair and crossing his legs. He wore an expensive tweed suit, white shirt and navy tie with discreet red stripes. He folded his hands in his lap.

Jessup threw him a quizzical look.

"In a manner of speaking," Guetz explained with a smile. "I'm assuming America has learned from her mistakes."

"I heard your speech this morning," Jessup said neutrally, reverting to the slow vowels of his native Texas. Something—call it instinct—signaled caution.

Guetz nodded. He twisted his head, inspecting the Fixer's office. He nodded appreciatively at the modern paintings and the Indo-Chinese sculptures the big man had collected. The rain clouds outside the plate glass windows were beginning to dissipate, and the needle-nosed tower of the Chrysler Building was dimly visible. "Quite some view. Looks like private consulting has been good to you, Walker. Real good."

"An American success story, General Guetz."

"Call me 'Harry,' Walker—it's a nickname. Hieronymous is too much of a mouthful. And my army career is a thing of the past. History, as they say these days."

Jessup smiled faintly at the intended pun. "Now what can I do for you?"

Guetz narrowed his eyes. He took a business card from his breast pocket and handed it across the desk. His name was printed in embossed letters. Underneath it were the words: Founder, Liberty Tribune.

"Little organization I and some interested parties put together a couple of years back. In the past we've concentrated on facilitating various...er...third-world development projects."

Jessup flicked the card back and forth with the edge of his thumb. "In other words, since Congress has rejected further military aid to the Nicaraguan Contras, you've been part of the effort to fund them privately." He smiled generously. "The Liberty Tribune isn't exactly a secret. Especially since the Sandinistas shot down that supply airplane."

The retired general shrugged. "We fight communism on all fronts. Actually we're scaling down our operations in Central America. Nicaragua has been a valuable opportunity to focus the public's attention, but it's never been much of a real threat. Let's face it. With America's military might, we can squash them like a bug when we have to. These days we raise funds for political campaigns, lobby congressmen. Eternal vigilance for freedom."

He lowered his eyes and stared at his clasped hands. "It's important." He looked up, right into Jessup's eyes. "We can't afford to have our efforts jeopardized by gung-ho idiots."

Jessup raised his brows. "I have a feeling this is where I come in."

Guetz turned, for a moment watching the clouds dissipate beyond the plate glass window. He turned back to Jessup, fidgeting slightly.

"I hear rumors, Walker. Stories that you got some people working for you. Professionals. Risk takers. Specialists in getting the job done quietly and efficiently and with a minimum amount of publicity."

Jessup stared at the general, his face impassive. Proceed with caution, he thought. His voice stayed even. "The intelligence community thrives on rumor, Harry. We both know that."

A slight smile played across the general's lips. Then he sighed and nodded. "Well, let's just leave that alone, then, and I'll tell you my problem. This morning I was given some information about someone in my organization. How is not important. You're aware that when the Ayatollah came to power in Iran, and the embassy was seized, the Carter administration stopped shipment on millions of dollars' worth of arms that Iran had already paid for?"

The Fixer nodded. "Still rotting in warehouses in New Jersey."

Guetz chuckled uncomfortably. "Iranians are real pissed off about it. Have been for years. Especially with this Iraqi war on their hands. They're desperate. They've had agents here in the States working for years on getting it out. Somewhere along the way, they approached one of my people through the guise of an Argentinean intermediary. Asked him to help them get the stuff to the freedom fighters in Central America. In fact, everything will go straight to Iran. My man is a real firebrand. And a patriot. He doesn't know he's being hoodwinked. Some of the people who are associated with our organization have connections right up to the White House. If he's caught, and the press makes the connection between him and the Liberty Tribune, it will be a scandal of major national concern. Our work is too important for that."

The Fixer sat back in his chair, crossing his hands nonchalantly behind his head. "You know how they plan on getting hold of these arms?"

"The arms are in a warehouse in a shipping yard on Newark Bay next to a dry dock where a Liberian freighter has just been refurbished. They plan on taking over the compound, locking up the guards, and loading the crates of weapons and ordnance on the freighter. By the time the sun rises, they'll be in international waters. It's a brilliant scheme."

"And when is all this supposed to take place?"

"Tonight. Midnight."

Jessup whistled. "That's cutting it very close. Why did they come to this man in your organization?"

"He has military experience. And they needed an American to get them through the gates." Guetz shrugged. "And I suppose Iranian intelligence saw it as a way of getting back at us for the arms scam last year. By implicating me."

"Who is he?"

General Guetz reached into his coat and withdrew a photograph from the inside pocket. He dropped it on the desk. Jessup didn't touch it. He just looked. It was Deke Howard.

The general was staring at Jessup, who nodded very slowly. "The *Callisto*."

"This man's had a difficult time adjusting since the war. Bit of a save-the-world complex. I offered him a job last year. Thought it might help him. He's got into this with some of his Legion buddies."

Walker Jessup flicked his eyes from the general's face to the face in the photograph. Evidently, Deke Howard wasn't the only one who thought he was going to save the world.

"Why haven't you stopped him yourself?" the Fixer asked tightly.

"I didn't find out until this morning, just before the parade. From an intelligence source in D.C. Deke is supposed to meet me this afternoon at our offices in the World Trade Center. I'm going to dissuade him from doing anything else. He's going to take a long trip to a faraway destination until the air clears. But that's not going to stop the Iranians."

"That's what you want me for."

"You—" the general nodded "—or the people who work for you." He stood. Once again, he reached inside his jacket. He took out an envelope and withdrew a thick wad of money. They were thousand-dollar bills. He placed it on the polished granite desk.

"Fifty thousand dollars. From my personal account, as a retainer. With an equal amount if the Iranians are stopped."

For a moment Jessup stared at it. He remembered the parade a few hours earlier, and the strange look on Nile Barrabas's face when General Guetz had stepped to the podium to begin his speech. In one respect, the Fixer and the warrior were exactly alike: neither man could resist the temptation of a dare. In this case, Jessup wondered how Barrabas would react to saving the general's ass. On the other hand, there was no need for Barrabas to know the identity of the client. Iranian secret agents were fair game.

The Texan stood, his plump hand covering the wad of currency and whisking it away.

"Plus expenses." He extended his hand. "I'll let you know what they come to."

The retired general grasped the proffered hand. "And no publicity."

"Guaranteed."

When Guetz was gone, Walker Jessup sat at his desk, staring at the pile of bank notes. He gave even odds that Hieronymous Guetz was hiding something. But information was the Fixer's most valuable asset. He had enough of it in his filing cabinets to sink the free world. He liked to think it was in safe hands. With his index finger he stabbed the button on the intercom.

"Jimmy, I want the files on the frozen Iranian arms shipments. And some maps of the New Jersey waterfront."

He looked at his watch. It was almost one. Barrabas telephoned every day promptly at two. That gave Walker just enough time for lunch. Then he and the man were going to jump the clock and pay an early visit to the New Jersey waterfront.

In the meantime, there was a great Irish pub just across Madison Avenue that served the best braised ribs in all of Manhattan. The fat Texan started salivating. He tucked the money into the top drawer. Bermuda and the chocolate chicken at La Guanillo would have to wait a few days, but what the hell. He worked hard for his money. And fifty thousand smackeroos was going to buy him one hell of a pigout.

3

Once the steady drizzle stopped, fresh Atlantic winds blew the heavy cloud cover aside, and the skies over Manhattan turned blue.

It was midafternoon. Nile Barrabas was waiting on the steps of his hotel. He wore chinos and a navy blue nylon windbreaker. His eyes followed with interest the green BMW swinging relentlessly around the fountain in Grand Army Plaza. Pedestrians scattered as the vehicle barreled through an intersection. The driver stomped on the brakes, and the expensive German car screeched to a halt before the hotel.

"Walker, as a driver you are ruthless," the warrior commented, climbing in beside the fat man and settling back in the leather-upholstered bucket seat.

Jessup shrugged. "New York is a perpetual battleground between people on foot and people in cars. There are no rules. There is only survival." He hit the gas, and the BMW shot into Fifty-ninth Street. A few minutes later, they were heading down Ninth Avenue.

"All you said on the phone was Iranian arms," Barrabas prompted. They joined the pileup of cars turning into the Lincoln Tunnel.

"The ones President Carter refused to ship after the hostages were seized in '79. They've been rotting in

New Jersey warehouses ever since. I got a hot tip from a prospective client that they're about to be tampered with. The Iranians want them for the Persian Gulf War real bad. It's worth a hundred thousand dollars to us, fifty for you, fifty for me. Not bad for a night's work, I figure.''

"Night?"

"That's when they're supposed to move the arms. I had a friend in the Pentagon pull some strings to get us a guided tour beforehand. I thought we'd drive out and poke around a bit. Bit of reconnaissance.''

"What makes you think I'll be interested? Fifty thousand is chicken feed compared to what Heinzmuller has salted away for me in Zurich.''

Jessup turned to look at Barrabas. The former army colonel was taunting him with a smile. It was true. The soldier had done very well for himself as a mercenary. He was worth millions.

"You mean you're not playing the market with all that moolah?''

Barrabas laughed. "Stocks? Yeah, they keep going up, and one of these days the bubble will burst and you'll all be smiling soap suds.''

The Fixer looked as disbelieving as possible. "Fine," he said, shrugging. "Say no."

Barrabas snickered and looked through the back windshield. Jessup had his number. All the Texan had to do was dangle the barest possibility of an adventure before his nose, and Barrabas was game. It was the old story of the mule and the carrot.

"I'm hooked," Barrabas replied, with an unrestrained smile.

The car entered the long white-tiled tunnel under the Hudson River. Twenty minutes later, the BMW was bouncing in and out of potholes. A crumbling road led through an industrial wasteland of factories and freeways and noxious sloughs where garbage floated on the surface of scum-filled ponds. The island of Manhattan, studded with towers of glass and stone, spread along the horizon across the river to the east, glittering and silent in the distance.

Heading south, they passed rows of warehouses and adjacent docks, some obviously in use, others seemingly abandoned. Rusting freighters waited in dry dock at the sides of rotting piers. Finally, flat grasslands on their right opened up to the New Jersey Turnpike, far to the west. On their left, on a long stretch of waterfront, was an industrial graveyard, where two-story mounds of ancient machinery rusted to oblivion. Beyond, rows of neat, well-kept warehouses with corrugated-metal roofs were lined up like military barracks, and surrounded by several perimeters of high-wire fences.

"Got a gun?" Jessup inquired.

Barrabas nodded once. He carried a standard military side arm, the Browning HP, in a holster inside his jacket.

"Use your fist and bang on the door panel just below the handle."

Barrabas followed Jessup's instructions, slamming his hand solidly against the door. The leather-lined panel along the bottom half of the door slid smoothly back, revealing an Uzi submachine gun clipped against the metal frame beside a neat row of spare magazines.

"Very clever."

"Very convenient," Jessup seconded. "I got an old Company buddy who runs a rifle range on the West Side. Very inventive fellow. Hit it again and it'll close. Thought I'd let you know, just in case."

The BMW came abreast of a guardhouse halfway down a half-mile stretch of ten-foot-high frost fence, which was topped with rows of barbed and razor wire. Small porcelain electrical conductors were perched at even intervals along an inner wire fence. Large signs exhibited red lightning bolts and warned in big black letters of mortal danger. Jessup turned into the drive and slowed beside the guard booth. He flashed an identification card. The guard, an older gray-haired man, his gun in an open holster, stepped from the booth and examined the card carefully, flicking his eyes back and forth from the photograph to Jessup's face several times. He wore a dark green uniform, with the crest of a private security agency on the shoulder.

"Dick Rebock here?" Jessup asked. The guard pointed to the first warehouse, which housed an office at one end.

"He's expecting you, Mr. Jessup."

They drove through and parked. Barrabas noted several armed guards patrolling between the rows of warehouses. Video surveillance cameras, mounted on the eaves of the buildings, were monitored by several men behind a large console in the office.

The Fixer and Barrabas had been greeted at the door by Dick Rebock, a friendly, garrulous man. He was an Army veteran who had grown an enormous paunch, and he managed the security at the warehouse compound. He shook hands with the two men. They declined his offer of coffee in favor of a fast tour of the compound.

There were a dozen warehouses, each half the size of a football field, lined up in two rows of six. At the end of the compound, three piers stretched into the waters of Newark Bay. Half a mile to the south, the chimney of a dry-dock foundry belched smoke, and the squawk and drum of cut-and-pounded steel drifted over them. An oceangoing freighter floated at anchor on the other side of a forest of rotting pylons that poked from the water. It sported a Liberian flag.

Barrabas exchanged glances with Jessup and nodded. Whoever the Fixer's mysterious client was, he was right about the freighter.

"Ah, it's just junk," Dick Rebock told them, oblivious to the silent language between the two men. He waved at the warehouses as they walked back through the compound. "Rocket and missile propellants are inert by now. That, or unstable. We've had leakages, too. Chemicals ate through the packing cases and seeped right into the concrete floor. Caused a helluva lot of damage." He shook his head, as if to say that someone somewhere was a real idiot.

"Who pays for all this?" Barrabas asked.

"The shah paid for it all. Hundreds of millions of dollars' worth of equipment. Then came the revolution. Carter stopped the shipment and impounded billions of dollars of Iranian money in bank accounts. That money earns interest, and the interest pays the storage charges, the damages and my salary. Hell, I set up this little security company after I left the Army—as a sideline, you know. Getting bored with my retirement. I'm a rich man now, thanks to the Ayatollah.''

"And all this stuff is useless?''

Rebock looked at Barrabas with big, skeptical eyes. "Let me tell you something. It's more than useless. It's downright dangerous. The fellow who goes in and tries to move this stuff, he's got to have definite suicidal tendencies. There are leaking acids in there that'll eat through human flesh in seconds."

"Do you get people poking around?''

Rebock laughed. "Maybe six times the surveillance cameras have picked up Iranian agents spying on us. We turn the tapes over to the FBI, and they're on the next flight back to Teheran. Nah, it's been quiet for the last year and a half or so. I figure they've about given up by now."

"They must know this equipment is useless," Barrabas said to Jessup. "The shelf life of these kind of armaments isn't classified."

Jessup nodded. He looked troubled.

The three men began walking toward the front of the compound where the BMW was parked.

"Now, down the road another half mile, on the other side of the dry dock, it's another story. Buddy of mine runs his own security company, too: he's in charge of that depot. It's the same as this place."

"Phil Kirby?"

"That's him. They had some kind of trouble a few weeks ago. Every day a car driving by, parking up in the grass and hanging around. Finally sent two of his boys out for a look-see. They got beat up real bad. But they weren't Iranians. Americans is what I heard. Duck hunters, I figure. We get lots of them around here, too, this time of year. It's out of season. Must have been a little tanked up and got scared when they saw the uniforms. 'Course that don't mean they can go 'round beating the shit outta folks. Messed up those guys real bad...."

Barrabas gave Jessup a friendly slap on his massive belly. "Check it out?"

The fat man nodded. They declined Rebock's offer of coffee again and walked toward the BMW.

"Was this next place on your list?" Barrabas asked.

Jessup nodded. "Yup. Duck hunters. What do you figure?" He paused for a moment. He hadn't told Barrabas the name of his client yet, or about Deke Howard's possible involvement.

Barrabas looked away, his gaze following a car that approached the compound on the other side of the wire fence. It was going quickly, bouncing up and down on the bruised and battered surface of the decaying street—an old station wagon painted camouflage green. He recognized it. The ersatz bamboo cage on the roof was gone, but it looked like the same car he'd seen at the Veterans Day parade barely six hours earlier. The car sped past the compound, heading farther along the waterfront. The professional soldier didn't believe in coincidence.

"C'mon, let's take a look," Barrabas said, moving quickly toward the BMW. They climbed into the car. Jessup drove through the gates of the compound and turned onto the crumbling industrial road. Barrabas slipped his hand inside his baggy nylon jacket and took out the Browning. He checked the clip and pushed the safety off.

Jessup cast a worried glance in his direction. "What's up?"

The station wagon had already disappeared.

"Hit it, Walker," Barrabas commanded.

The urgency in the warrior's voice was persuasive. Jessup floored the accelerator, and the BMW lurched wildly down the road while he made vain attempts to miss the yard-wide craters that cracked its surface.

The next warehouse depot was much smaller than the first, with six long wide metal buildings facing one another in two rows of three. A street ran at right angles to the main road inside the perimeter fence and led between the two warehouses to the waterfront. Barrabas spotted a small tugboat tied up at a pier on the other side of the compound. There was activity—men loading crates. Several cars were parked in front of the last warehouse. The guard post was located three quarters of the way down the quarter-mile length of the perimeter fence. A driveway spanned a shallow ditch about thirty feet long. Jessup turned into it and slammed on the brakes in front of the tiny guard-house. The front gates were closed but didn't appear to be locked.

"Is the windshield bulletproof?" Barrabas asked.

Jessup nodded dumbly, feeling the tension of the unknown uncoil mysteriously in his stomach. The mercenary's instincts were going full tilt, and in this situation, the Fixer trusted them more than his own.

The fact that Barrabas was still alive after all these years, all those wars, was proof enough that he could be relied on.

The Texan rolled down the window, flashing his identification card with one hand. No guard appeared. He peered through the obscure shadows inside the guardhouse. What looked to be a foot, toe up, was barely visible within.

"What's going on?" Barrabas demanded sharply.

Jessup leaned farther out.

A rivulet of bright red blood wound its way from under the guardhouse door and snaked across the concrete foundation pad, draining into the gravel beneath the tires of the BMW.

He dropped back inside the car, his face white. "We're in a shitload of trouble!"

"WAIT HERE," Deke Howard told the driver, who parked the station wagon next to two late-model black Fords outside the open doors of the last warehouse. A third Ford, the one that had escorted them from the front gates, pulled up beside them. Howard stepped out and slammed the door shut, surveying the scene. He was decked out in loden-green and tawny camouflage gear from head to foot, including the rebel cap he wore over his brown hair. He walked slowly toward a group of six men standing nearby. Most of them were in dark bulky clothing. Some wore sunglasses.

As far as Deke knew, they were Nicaraguans, former members of Anastasio Somoza's virulent National Guard, and now part of the Contra forces fighting against the Sandinistas. They had flown in from Miami that morning. Most of them were armed with automatic weapons.

He paused, scratching at the two-day growth of beard on his thin face. The submachine guns weren't necessary. He had made the appropriate arrangements for the removal of the matériel. Another half-dozen men were on the rotting pier, hurriedly loading crates of explosives and ammunition onto the tug.

Phil Kirby, an old army buddy from Vietnam days who now ran the security at the depot, was vehemently arguing with the group on the pier, his hands flailing as he gesticulated wildly. He looked worried and angry. The leader of the Nicaraguans appeared unconcerned, even bored. Kirby saw Howard approaching and put up his hands to stop the conversation. He strode out of hearing distance toward his old friend. A signal, unobserved by the Americans, passed silently among the aliens.

"Deke, what in hell's going on?" Kirby demanded. "You told me this Iranian stuff was going to help freedom fighters in Central America. Half these guys don't even speak Spanish. What's with the gun toting? And what's the idea of rounding up all my men and putting them inside the warehouse?"

Howard nodded slowly, looking carefully around the depot. The group of Nicaraguans was breaking up, the men fanning out. Something was wrong. Goddamn Latinos, why don't they just do what we planned on, he thought.

"I'll talk to them," he told Kirby. The Nicaraguan leader was eyeing them carefully. Howard motioned to Kirby, and the two Americans walked toward the warehouse. They had barely taken a step when they heard a harsh shout behind them.

Three of the so-called Nicaraguans stood behind them, their automatic rifles pointed at their backs. Another man opened the door of the station wagon and pulled the driver from his seat, pushing him against the car and frisking him. The foreigners shouted, motioning with the barrels of their guns toward the warehouse. And it wasn't Spanish.

"What in hell—" Deke Howard had barely opened his mouth when the men rushed him and Kirby, shoving them brusquely forward, punching them with rifles and yelling in some incomprehensible language. The "Contra" leader stood silently nearby, observing with a benign smile.

Howard swung around to grab the stock of the rifle that prodded him in the back. The Contra stepped sideways and swung the weapon hard into his solar plexus. Howard gasped, the excruciating pain flooding his torso and driving the air from his diaphragm.

The Contras jabbered at each other as they herded the three Americans through the open door of the warehouse. Kirby slipped his arm under Howard's shoulder and lifted him, helping his friend to walk.

Inside the cold, dank building, long shadowy rows of wooden crates were stacked fifteen feet high in cantilevered bins. A dozen or so men in the blue uniforms of Kirby's security company were lined up facing the front wall, their hands in the air. Three of the Nicaraguans stood, legs planted wide apart, fifteen feet behind them. Cold terror sank deep into Deke Howard's soul. It was a firing squad.

"No!" he screamed hoarsely, still heaving for air.

Orange muzzle-flash exploded from the barrels of the submachine guns. Brass shell casings sputtered and popped, pinging onto the concrete floor. The flesh ripped open across the backs of the security guards, and they tumbled like bloody ten pins in a bowling alley.

JESSUP FLOORED the gas pedal and banged his fist against the door. The fuel-injected BMW surged forward, slamming through the unlocked gates. The panel slid back, revealing a second Uzi carefully concealed in the metal framework. Barrabas was there ahead of him. He ripped the other Uzi from the clips that held it to the door and slammed a forty-round magazine into it. He rolled down the window and leaned over the edge.

Jessup veered left inside the gate, accelerated along the side of the first long warehouse and swung the steering wheel sharply to the right. The tires of the BMW squealed loudly in a controlled fishtail. The car was on the main road that ran between the two rows of warehouses to the waterfront.

The vicious chatter of automatic weapons broke from the last warehouse. Armed men standing outside the open doors turned at the sound of the rapidly approaching BMW. They raised their guns.

Barrabas squeezed the trigger of the Uzi. The compact SMG spat bullets at a rate of six hundred and fifty rounds a minute. The Israeli submachine gun bounced against the side of the car with the recoil. Crossing his left hand over, he grasped the back of the metal stock to steady it. Spent shell casings, caught in the wind stream of the fast-moving car, chunked against the roof and rear windows.

The men outside the warehouse returned fire, and the windshield shattered into a row of spiderwebs. The bullets ricocheted harmlessly off the thick bullet-proof glass. The car wove from side to side. Jessup gripped the steering wheel tightly with his right hand, fighting against a skid. With his left, he held the Uzi out the window and squeezed the trigger.

"Yeee-haw!" he let out a Texan cowboy whoop. The velocity of the car and the recoil almost tore the gun from his hand. The men in front of the warehouse fled toward the pier. One tumbled as he caught a handful of 9 mm parabellum from Barrabas's gun and went down. A second turned to fire back. His face exploded into gore. He flew into the air, stretched horizontally and landed, spread-eagled and dead.

Deke Howard and Phil Kirby stumbled madly from the warehouse, calmly pursued by three of the aliens. Two saw the BMW racing blindly toward them, muzzle fire flashing from both sides. Their faces frozen in horror, they jumped over the fallen bodies of their comrades and hightailed it for the tugboat. The third one hesitated, swinging his automatic rifle toward the two fleeing Americans. Three rounds punched into Kirby's back, arching him forward, his knees collapsing beneath the weight of his lifeless body. The alien turned toward Howard and aimed.

Barrabas saw the man in camouflage fatigues rolling on the ground away from the warehouse. He stretched farther out the window, gripping the Uzi carefully with one hand and firing off a short burst across the hood of the speeding car. The parabellum punched into the alien's chest, lifting him into the air and throwing him back into the warehouse.

On the dock, a man rapidly uncoiled the mooring rope and threw it onto the tug. The stack belched dirty black diesel fumes. The fleeing aliens raced along the rotting planks as the boat drew away from the side of the pier. They leapt across the widening gap. Three made it. The fourth came in short, his hands scraping the side of the deck. Several men ran forward and pulled him over as the boat cleared the end of the pier.

"Yee-haw!" Jessup screamed again, steering the BMW straight up the road toward the pier and letting off another burst from his SMG. Both men aimed for the deck of the tug. Their fire pounded harmlessly against the wooden tug, sending showers of splinters into the water. The men on board raced to the stern and knelt behind a bulkhead. More bullets spattered against the BMW's cracked windshield, and the disintegrating glass bubbled inward.

"Whooa!" Jessup shouted. He pulled his arm in and threw the Uzi aside, gripping the steering wheel with his left hand. He took his foot off the accelerator and pulled on the parking brake. The BMW fishtailed three hundred and sixty degrees in a moonshiner's turn, throwing the two men back in their seats. Bullets punched into the side of the car.

"Hooowheee!" Jessup screamed over the numbing squeal of rubber tires on asphalt. He released the parking brake and hit the gas again. The BMW sped to cover on the other side of the warehouse and came to a halt.

In the instant of abrupt silence that followed, Barrabas and Jessup looked at each other. Then Barrabas yanked the door open and jumped out. The man in fatigues was picking himself slowly up from the ground. Barrabas recognized the face. It was Deke Howard. The mercenary's surprise faded as he noticed the panic in the man's eyes.

"It's wired to blow!" Howard screamed, running toward the car. "Get out! Get out!"

The mercenary opened the rear door and Deke Howard dove into the back seat like a swimmer off the starting box. The BMW was already gathering speed as Barrabas stepped inside. They had gone barely a hundred feet when the first of the explosions blasted away the front of the warehouse.

The shock waves pounded against the car. An enormous tongue of flame licked across the road, consuming the corpses scattered in front. A second explosion rocked the fleeing BMW. Red-hot metal debris battered the roof.

"Let's get out of here," Barrabas said to Jessup calmly in a low, even voice. "The whole place is going to go up."

He turned to look through the rear window. A great mushroom ball of liquid fire rose above the depot. The

warehouse disintegrated into millions of tiny fragments, and a rain of red-hot metal fell on the New
Jersey waterfront.

4

Nile Barrabas balled his fist tightly around Jessup's necktie, his knuckles pressing into his Adam's apple. He slammed the Texan up against the plate glass window, staring hard into his eyes and speaking furiously through clenched teeth.

"Don't you ever, ever screw me again, fat man."

Jessup fought to breathe against the pressure of the mercenary's fist on his larynx. His eyes darted sideways, catching a view out of the sixty-fourth-floor window. Dusk was gathering, and Manhattan's skyscrapers had lit up like a galaxy of stars. The glass seemed very thin.

"You got it?" Barrabas roared again. He pulled Jessup forward and slammed him against the window for the second time. The glass shivered. Jessup's face turned red with mortal fear.

"Stop," he gasped, his plump hands kneading desperately at Barrabas's fist. His face quickly turned crimson. "I got it," he croaked. "Never again!"

Barrabas gripped tighter and slammed the Texan against the window for the third time. The plate glass quivered harder. "Say it!" he shouted furiously.

"Never again!" Jessup's voice was painfully hoarse.

Barrabas let go.

The Fixer slumped to the floor, frantically pulling against the knot of his tie and ripping open his collar. The little button popped across the room. His chest heaved as he gasped for air. He had known that Barrabas was going to be pissed off when he was told the identity of Jessup's mysterious client, but he hadn't expected the murderous vengeance that had flooded into the warrior's ice-blue eyes. Slowly the blood drained from Jessup's head, and his color began to return to normal.

The white-haired warrior spun around to face the second man in the Fixer's office. Deke Howard sat in a chrome-and-leather chair, hunched forward, his face white with horror, his head slumped over his chest. He had been inarticulate since their narrow escape from the conflagration on the New Jersey waterfront.

"A lot of goddamn funny things happening today, Deke," Barrabas said to the silent man coldly. He grabbed a chair from its place against the wall, spun it around and sat on it the wrong way, leaning his elbows on its back. He was only a few feet away from the Vietnam veteran. He looked grim.

"We don't see each other in twelve years, and then twice in one day, you turn up in the wrong place at a bad time. Maybe you better start filling me in on what's happening."

Deke Howard swallowed and cocked his head, not daring to look up at the terrible wrath in the big man's eyes.

"Colonel," he said, barely audibly. It was Barrabas's last military rank, the rank he held when Deke

Howard had been a lieutenant in the 17th Waterborne Assault Group and commander of the *Callisto*. He coughed to clear his throat. "I dunno... Something went wrong. I—" he started uncertainly and stopped, his mind clouded by confusion. His voice was low and strangely lifeless.

"Whiskey," Barrabas ordered, turning to Jessup. The fat man, still wide-eyed with fear, nodded eagerly and pushed his vast flabby bulk up from the carpet. He lumbered over to a walnut credenza. A softly lit compartment held glasses and several bottles of expensive liquor. He poured a finger's breadth into a glass and handed it to Barrabas. Deke Howard took it eagerly and swallowed it in one gulp. Jessup turned back to the credenza and poured a second glass. He looked at it, debating, then decided and poured out more. He threw back the fiery amber liquid and shook his head as it went down. It helped.

Still seated, Barrabas handed Deke's empty glass to Jessup. The Fixer refilled it. This time Howard sipped.

"Now I want to hear it slow," Barrabas commanded. "From the beginning. One thing at a time."

The Vietnam veteran appeared thoughtful for a moment, fishing among his memories for the right place to start.

"I guess the beginning is when I got back from Nam," he said. He stopped again, remembering, and the pain was clearly evident on his face. "Because Nam was the end of the everything."

In a low, listless voice, separated from emotion, his gaze wandering along the floor of the room, the veteran told his story. It never quite made sense to him.

One day he was carrying body bags onto a patrol boat—all that was left of a platoon he'd delivered that morning. Someone handed him his papers, and two days later he stepped off the airplane in Hawaii, ordered a Big Mac and watched bikini-clad women on Waikiki Beach, as though nothing had ever happened. He returned to his hometown on Long Island, a vision of America that was picture perfect, a pretty wife, a baby son, the job his father-in-law had saved for him at the family's car dealership.

Then the nightmares started. First every once in a while, later nightly, then over and over again every night. He had no tolerance for annoyances. Anything could set him off: a careless comment at a bowling party, or being cut off by a thoughtless driver in traffic. And it wasn't just anger. It was rage. He wanted to destroy things. To kill people.

Drinking helped a little, dulled his sensitivity to minor disruptions. But then one night he woke up, gripped by a nightmare, plowing his fist into his pretty wife's face. She urged him to see a doctor. He did, but nothing seemed to stop what was roiling inside him.

His son was only a couple of years old. One day, at a family picnic, the little boy spilled his soft drink, and his father reacted by slugging him. He couldn't bear the thought of it happening again. His family was supportive, but he moved out the next day. When he came to visit, the little boy burst into tears and hid behind his mother, terrified of the strange monster who was his father.

"Haven't seen them now in years," Deke said. "She got married again. Guess his new dad is okay."

He drifted from city to city, he told Jessup and Barrabas. He could never sit still, never hold down a job for more than a few months at a time. He had no friends. Women he only used for sexual release. He was numb. He had no feelings, no emotions left. Occasionally, his drunken rages led to a destructive binge, and he spent time in jail. Afterward he'd get a hold on things and check into the psychiatric ward of a VA hospital. He never stayed more than a week or two.

"Posttraumatic stress disorder," Jessup murmured quietly. He had taken a chair near Barrabas and listened intently. "A lot of vets from that war have it. What they endured was so incredible. And we weren't even officially at war. They came home from hell and were expected to settle back into nice, honest lives. It's no wonder they had a hard time."

"That's it." Deke nodded. "That's what they told me at the VA hospitals. But it never seemed to get better. Two years ago, I came back here," he continued in a weary monotone. "Heard there was a good doctor out on Long Island, good at this kind of stuff. He put me in a support group of other veterans. For the first time since Nam, I felt I was getting better. I got a job. It wasn't much, pushing buttons at an automatic car wash, but I was making my own money again, and I stuck with it six months. Thought about going back to school. Maybe see my son again. Then everything fell apart again. I don't know why. The doctor told me relapses were, well, almost normal, that I should stick with him. But, Colonel—"

Deke Howard stopped abruptly, his voice almost cracking. He breathed harshly, fighting to regain control of his emotions. Finally Howard lifted his gaze and gave Barrabas a tentative look, then immediately cast his eyes back to the floor as if he were ashamed.

"Colonel, I didn't think I could take it anymore. I didn't believe it anymore, that anything would ever change. I went out, bought a gun—"

Again Howard stopped, the memory too painful to continue.

"To kill yourself?" Barrabas inquired softly. The hard, cold look had filtered from his eyes, replaced now by something close to understanding.

Deke nodded. A tear curled at the corner of one eye, and he brushed it quickly away. "Then I got the offer from the general," he piped up.

"General Guetz?"

Howard nodded, almost enthusiastically.

"How'd he find you?"

"One of the guys in the support group belonged to a veterans' chapter. The general had some connection to it through a guy who'd worked for him in Nam. He came to me—after all those years he remembered me from the mission up the Kap Long. That felt good, y'know. Having someone remember what you'd done. No one else does, here."

"You went to work for him?"

Again Deke Howard nodded. He raised his head and straightened in the chair as a small happy smile floated on his face. "Yeah. For the Liberty Tribune, actually. He told me I was needed in the fight against communism, y'know, and I thought, yeah, well, we lost over there in Southeast Asia, and it was my chance to do something about it."

He stopped, searching Barrabas's face for a glimmer of support.

"Y'know, it's like all those guys died for nothing. Friends of mine. Good men. What did they die for, if we don't...if we let..."

"That's what the general told you," Barrabas prompted.

Deke nodded, a little reluctantly. "Yeah, well, I think I always thought that. But it was like he knew how to say it. He used to talk to me, and somehow after listening to him, everything made sense finally."

"Now what about what happened in New Jersey today?"

Deke's face collapsed, and he buried it in his hands. "My God, my God, my God," he murmured. "What in hell went wrong?" Suddenly he stood, hyperventilating heavily, his eyes blind with desperation. He groped for the door, knocking into the chair and bumping against the wall. Barrabas stood, grabbing him quickly with a hand on each shoulder. He held Deke tightly against the wall at arm's length.

"It's okay, Deke. It's okay. You're with me now. I'm going to take care of it. All right?"

Howard looked at Barrabas, debate raging within him. Slowly his breathing subsided.

"All right?" Barrabas reiterated.

Deke nodded slowly. The colonel pushed him gently back into the chair.

"Now tell me what happened. Slowly, step by step."

"Those guys approached me, the ones back there at the warehouse."

"Why you, Deke?"

The veteran shrugged, shaking his head. He looked from Barrabas to Jessup, mystified. "I dunno. Because of the Liberty Tribune, I guess. We do a lot of business with the freedom fighters in Central America. These ones were part of a secret paramilitary operation training in Florida. They claimed to know some of the leaders of the Contra forces. Sure as hell knew all the names and everything."

"Do you speak Spanish, Deke?" Barrabas asked.

The veteran shook his head. "But it didn't sound much like Spanish back there in New Jersey," he said in a low voice, hanging his head.

"So, go on."

"They wanted those Iranian arms for the Nicaraguan freedom fighters, and somehow they knew Phil Kirby was an old army buddy. He had gambling debts, too. Atlantic City. He needed money. I talked him into it. It's my fault. Damn, it's all my fault." Once again, Deke Howard shrank forward in the chair, burying his face in his hands. There was an uncomfortable silence in the room. Barrabas leaned forward from his chair and patted him on the shoulder.

"It's okay, Deke. You got suckered. That's all. You can't blame yourself just because you survived."

Deke Howard sat up and looked the colonel hard in the eyes, the pain he felt replaced by anger that came close to simmering rage. In a tight-lipped voice he said, "Why not? It's what I been doing since that goddamn war ended. Blaming myself for surviving when all those good men died. Why the hell not? Who gave me the right to survive? Tell me!" His voice rose to hover on the verge of hysteria. "Tell me!" he demanded. "Why in hell—"

"Shut up, Deke!" Barrabas shouted harshly, cutting him off.

The veteran slumped back in his chair, turning away with a look of defeat.

"What now?" Jessup asked Barrabas softly.

"You ought to bloody well know—you're the damn Fixer!" Barrabas sneered.

Jessup winced. "Sorry. Just asking," he said with a tinge of sarcasm.

Barrabas put his hand to his forehead, massaging his temples and rubbing his eyes. Why does this make me feel so blasted tired? he thought. Like I haven't slept in two weeks? He sighed, standing and pushing the chair away.

"Next I go to see the general," he told them. And to himself he thought, just like I did thirteen years ago....

SAIGON. A HOT STEAMY DAY in 1974, the kind of smothering oppressive heat that pressed in, making breathing difficult, movement an effort. The stifling climate of that godforsaken land imitated the war that ravaged it, closing in like a claustrophobic's nightmare. Colonel Nile Barrabas, Military Attaché Liaison Office, Military Assistance Command—MAC— was sprawled across the bed, sweating profusely in the unrelenting humidity.

The alarm clock said seven-thirty. He drifted in the half world between sleep and waking, but even there, his mind focused on his work. For almost a year Bar-

rabas had been working military intelligence angles in
Saigon. In that time, he had never seen anything as
puzzling as the documents that had been brought into
MAC headquarters the day before. They had been
captured from an overrun bunker of the North Vietnamese Army—NVA—on the Ho Chi Minh trail by
some paratroopers with the Fifth Airborne. The papers had been damaged by fire, and experts at MAC
had begun the slow, painstaking task of reassembling
the crisp, charred fragments. So far, the partial picture they had assembled was uncharacteristic.
Abruptly, he opened his eyes and stared at the ceiling.
He had the answer.

The telephone on the bedside table jangled with
shrill persistent rings. Barrabas stretched out, grabbed
the phone and brought it to his ear, swallowing to clear
the phlegm that had gathered in his throat during his
few scant hours of sleep, and tried to sound as wide
awake as possible.

"Colonel?" a young man asked in the broad sliding nuances of a South Carolina accent. It was his
aide, Lieutenant Johnson. "You asked me to call as
soon as we got the word from Washington on your
request for a transfer to active duty. The telex came in
overnight."

Barrabas sat up, instantly alert. "And?"

"Negative, sir. They turned it down. I'm sorry.
There's more. They kinda like what you're doing at
MAC. Do you want me to read it to you?"

Barrabas exhaled heavily, with a crushing sense of
disappointment. "Never mind, Johnson. I'll be in in

half an hour. I want to go over those captured NVA documents again.''

''Bin Doc's already at it, sir. The translations are almost finished.''

''Good. I'll be there in twenty minutes.''

He dropped the telephone onto its cradle and slumped back against the headboard. A ceiling fan circled lazily overhead, and from the street the noises of gathering traffic drifted in with the sweltering heat. Screwed, chewed and goosed, he thought. It had all the logic of army life. Do a good job in the field, and they reward you with a desk at the Pentagon. Beg and plead to get back to the front line, and they assign a job where the most strenuous work involves gathering intelligence on the embassy cocktail circuit. That's what the Military Attaché Liaison Office was all about.

He pushed himself out of bed, then trotted over to stand naked in front of the bathroom mirror and turned on the cold water faucet. At six foot two, his war-hardened body towered over the sink. On his thigh, his rib cage, his shoulder, neck and upper arm, the thin twisted lines of white scar tissue contrasted against his deeply tanned skin.

The places where the bullets had gone in. Like worm holes in polished wood, he thought. There was a place-name and a date for every mark, and usually a medal to go along with it. What was it now? Two Silver Stars and a Distinguished Service Cross. He'd left off counting the Purple Hearts.

He was young, decorated—they called him a hero— and he was one of the most rapidly promoted officers in the United States military. He brushed his hand through his thick chestnut-brown hair, noting that it needed trimming before lunch. He stuck his hand in the sink. The water was more tepid than cold.

Could be worse, he thought. At least I'm not shuffling papers behind a desk at the Pentagon. He splashed handfuls on his face, wiping the sleep from his eyes, then grabbed his razor.

A few minutes later, he climbed into the car that took him to MAC headquarters, a small two-story building on the grounds of the U.S. embassy compound. Somehow, the free associations that came easily during the rise from deep sleep to wakefulness had brought the persistent memory of a seemingly unrelated incident to mind.

The previous week he had spent an evening at a long dull dinner party at the Hungarian embassy. It was standard MAC intelligence duty. The foreign embassies of the war-torn capital were rife with rumors that ranged from the ridiculous to the inane. But occasionally tidbits of valuable information seeped through.

Halfway through the evening, the Hungarian ambassador made his way across the crowded room. The young colonel stood alone, leaning against the mantel of a fireplace and sipping his coffee. The portly dark-haired man teased Barrabas about opposition to the war in America. With an insidious smile, the plump ambassador added, "Sometimes the Vietcong always seem to know your every move. Their intelligence is very good, do you not think?" The diplomat shrugged carelessly. "But to ask such a question is to suggest impossible answers." He had smiled with mock generosity and faded into the glittering crowd without waiting for a response.

The impossible answer, Barrabas mused grimly, returning to the present and stepping from the car to enter MAC headquarters, was very possible indeed. He made his way quickly to the laboratory at the back of the building, knocking when his saw the red light over the door. A voice shouted for him to enter.

In the darkened room, Bin Doc stood out in his white lab coat. He was moving a shallow basin back and forth with his hands, bathing a photographic plate gently in a chemical solution. Developed prints hung to dry on a line across the worktable. Lieutenant Johnson was peering at them, reading by the glow of the dim red overhead light.

"I have just finished," the Vietnamese scientist said, lifting the final photograph from the solution. He turned on a water faucet to rinse the setting solution off.

"The radioactive isotopes worked like a charm, sir," Johnson told him. "We can read those documents from these photographs as if they'd never been burned."

Bin Doc clipped the last photograph to the line and turned on a desk light.

"They're maps!" Barrabas exclaimed, seeing the crudely drawn lines clearly on the drying paper.

"Of the Mekong Delta, Colonel," Bin Doc said. He pointed to certain features and rhymed off the American names. Barrabas followed carefully, his uneasiness building. Every American and South Vietnamese army outpost, landing zone and supply depot over hundreds of square miles had been carefully marked.

"What's this say?" Barrabas pointed to the Vietnamese characters surrounding a chopper supply base at Ke Dong.

As Bin Doc hesitated uncomfortably, Lieutenant Johnson took the plunge. "Troop strengths. Artillery. Length of perimeter lines." The lieutenant moved his finger over the photographs. Every military installation in the area had been similarly detailed. "How in hell do they get that kind of information, sir?"

Barrabas left the question unanswered. "What about this writing, Bin Doc?" He pointed to columns of Vietnamese characters that ran down the left side of several of the documents.

"Is further information," the scientist replied, scrunching his forehead and narrowing his eyes to peer at the tiny, hastily written calligraphy. "In Vietnamese, but it's all wrong."

"How do you mean, wrong?"

"The syntax," Bin Doc stated. "This has been done in a great haste. And whoever wrote it, sometimes he writes as if he were Vietnamese, but in other places, the word order is all wrong. As if, perhaps, he was writing English but using Vietnamese idioms."

"Or translating?" Lieutenant Johnson suggested.

Barrabas snapped out his orders. "Bin Doc, translate." He tapped the oddly written material. "Lieutenant, run some of this information through unit command to see how accurate it is."

"It's classified information, Colonel. They'll be reluctant to even confirm it upstairs."

"If it's accurate, we'll have internal investigations breathing down our neck within hours. One way or another, we'll know."

Two hours later, Colonel Barrabas was on the carpet in front of his commanding officer, General Walter Hangroy, a tall, needle-thin Oklahoma native with distinguished gray hair.

"You almost caused a riot at unit command," Hangroy murmured, staring at the photographs on his desk. "No one is supposed to have this kind of information outside of Joint Command. You know what that means?"

The colonel nodded. "A spy."

Hangroy dropped the photos and looked up. "And probably an imminent NVA offensive against our troops in the Mekong."

"Who's in charge there—that's General Guetz, isn't it?" Barrabas said, answering his own question.

"Hieronymous, or Harry, Guetz, affectionately known as General Blood and Guts to his men," Hangroy confirmed. "This is good work, Nile. We have two priorities. Reestablishing our defenses in the Mekong and rooting out the source of this material."

He glanced at his watch. "Coincidentally, I'm due at a luncheon at the Majestic Hotel for a general visiting from the Pentagon. Harry Guetz is one of the guests."

"You'll talk to him?"

Hangroy shook his head. "Uh-uh. You will." He stood up and reached for his jacket on the nearby coatrack. A look of dismay crossed Barrabas's face, and Hangroy looked sympathetic.

"I know. You'd rather chew bullets. But since this has come up, they want me at Joint Command. You'll have to stand in for me. You're entitled to take a guest, too. At least you'll get to eat. I have a feeling I'll be in meetings for the next two days as a result of this."

Several hours later, Colonel Barrabas and Lieutenant Johnson were trotting up the steps of the elegant old Majestic Hotel. Their dress uniforms were already soiled with sweat, another example of the seemingly endless futility in the war-torn country. "I feel like a spare prick at a whore's wedding, sir. So to speak," the young lieutenant muttered darkly as they entered the air-conditioned comfort of the hotel's lobby.

Barrabas grinned at the South Carolinian's colorful speech. "It's an order, Johnson. I need someone sane to talk to."

Lunch was a supposedly impromptu birthday celebration for the visiting general. As the two men approached the doors to the private dining room, another lieutenant was exiting. For a split second he tried to avoid Johnson's glance of recognition. It was too late.

"Dale Switzer!" Johnson called to him, proffering his hand.

The other lieutenant turned to nod a dark greeting. His face was streaked with livid pink scar tissue, fresh from a recent wound. He shook hands.

Lieutenant Johnson tried not to stare. "Are you a prisoner of lunch, too?" he joked to hide his discomfort.

Lieutenant Switzer didn't smile. "No. I merely conveyed General Guetz's regrets to the hosts and the guest of honor. He's been called away on an urgent matter on short notice."

Barrabas and Johnson exchanged glances. Both knew what the urgent matter entailed. The lieutenant with the scarred face pushed past them without a further word, heading for the front doors of the hotel.

"I went to the academy with him," Johnson said, staring after the departing man. "I'd heard he'd run into a Cong booby trap a few months back. Now he's working for old Blood and Guts himself."

"And our sole reason for being here vanishes." Barrabas sighed, but it was too late to back out.

Lunch was long and dull. A dozen high-ranking Vietnamese generals had flown in from the field to meet the American general. Several high-ranking American officers were also present. Conversation up and down the long table centered on the war.

If for nothing else, Barrabas had to admire the South Vietnamese generals for their perseverance. They were within a hairline of winning, they emphasized. With perhaps a few more divisions of American soldiers, a few more hundred million dollars' worth of aid, the borders would be stabilized. "Isn't that right, Colonel Barrabas?" they'd inquire gently, in hopes of a rhetorical answer.

His reply was noncommittal. What the war lacked was what no one dared say out loud. It lacked a genuine cause. Somehow, in the politics and confusion, the futility and frustration, the endless statistics on body counts and defoliated forests, the incredible absence of real motivation on the part of simple infantry soldiers—American or Vietnamese—was entirely overlooked. Had any of these generals been in the field, he wondered. It was like a zoo out there.

"And, of course," a Vietnamese general said between sips of coffee from a gold-rimmed cup, "we support the efforts of your government to Vietnamize the war, but we need more time to train officers and soldiers. You must convince your secretary of defense of this."

"This is very important." A general named Tran Phan Dong spoke up, raising a glass of liqueur to his thin lips. "These students and hippies, as you call them in your country, they have conspired with the press to halt the American war effort. They have betrayed us. I do not understand why your government puts up with it." He balled his hand into a fist and pounded on the white linen tablecloth. "They are the real traitors to our glorious cause. They should be crushed."

Colonel Barrabas felt his memory nudged by General Tran's disagreeable comments; he remembered the comment the Hungarian ambassador had made at the embassy cocktail party the night before, and the evidence of espionage he had just uncovered.

Suddenly Barrabas made a connection to the mysterious papers. Like a bolt of lightning, the impossible answer came.

He nudged Lieutenant Johnson with his elbow.

"Let's get out of here," he whispered to his aide, rising from the table and apologizing to the other guests. They walked quickly through the richly paneled doors and stepped into the hotel lobby. The young lieutenant stopped, quickly patting his breast pockets.

"My pen. I left it on the table. It was a present from my wife," he explained with a guilty grimace. "She'd kill me."

The colonel nodded. The lieutenant strode back through the doors into the private dining room just as the bomb under the long table exploded.

One of the thick wooden doors smacked into Barrabas like a giant paddle, lifting him off his feet and hurling him against a marble column in the hotel lobby. Shattered glass tinkled and fell, and there were thuds of falling plaster and partitions. The air was filled with dust and flying debris. There was a stunned silence. Then groans. Screams. A warm wet rain spattered down on him. He opened his eyes. It was blood. Flesh and blood.

Barrabas kicked away the broken door that had fallen across the lower half of his body and jumped to his feet, feeling a bruising pain up one side of his body. The billowing clouds of plaster dust began to settle. He ran forward, staring in horror.

He stood amidst a field of dismembered naked limbs whose severed veins still spurted blood, and ragged bits of unidentifiable flesh—all that was left of the general's impromptu birthday party. At that moment began the most bizarre and senseless journey of his life.

5

Night had fallen when Barrabas flagged a taxi on Madison Avenue. He gave the driver an East Village address on Avenue A.

"Alphabet City?" The man nodded. "Shuah. Why not. Some drivers wouldn't take you ta that neighborhood. But a buck's a buck, I always say." The driver shot into the fast-moving traffic and headed downtown.

"Rush, rush, rush," the cabdriver chanted, throwing his arms into the air and letting the steering wheel fend for itself for a few seconds. "But I ask you, where's everyone going?"

"Same place as you and me," Barrabas responded, grinning ruefully at the driver's simple philosophy.

The talkative driver grabbed the wheel again but jabbed at the air with his finger. "Well said, my man, well said." He continued the attempt to engage his fare in conversation, but gave up after a series of monosyllabic answers.

Barrabas settled back in his seat, forbidding the return of those memories from the awful Asian war. It was something Deke Howard had unwittingly expressed very well. Everything started in Vietnam, because Vietnam was the end of everything. The bullet at Kap Long that had pierced his helmet and come fractions of an inch from turning him into a permanent vegetable, for example. Must have been that bullet that turned his hair white, the doctors said. But correlation was not causation. No one knew the whole story. The amnesia, for example, had only been temporary. By the time his memory returned in the Saigon hospital, he was savvy enough to keep his mouth shut. The ignorance of the doctors had probably saved his life in the years since. But now it looked as if the debts had come due.

The cab swung around Union Square and turned onto Fourteenth Street, coasting past the discount stores, boarded up theaters and fast-food joints that led to the Puerto Rican neighborhoods on the east side of Manhattan. Despite the grime and apparent poverty, there was at least a semblance of family life here: mothers with strollers, kids hanging around outside the video parlors, gangs of adolescent boys and girls flirting capriciously.

At Thompkins Square Park, the street life began to change. Stylishly dressed men and women swarmed in and out of white-walled art galleries, neon signs glowed in restaurant windows and punks paraded at the edge of the park, panhandling. Bag people in rags permeated with the stench of excrement rummaged through garbage cans with the delicacy of small animals, looking for a few morsels of something to eat.

"Right there—" Barrabas tapped against the window, indicating the corner of Seventh Street. He paid the driver and hopped across the detritus in the gutter to stand on the cracked and broken sidewalk.

Squeezed narrowly between a mom-and-pop coffee shop with laminated plastic counters and a chic restaurant with a Hawaiian name was a remnant of what New York once was: a hole-in-the-wall newspaper stand and dairy counter.

Wood racks outside the front window held stacks of newspapers in half a dozen languages, and a tattered green awning advertised egg creams and chocolate malts. People passing by grabbed copies of the *Times*, the *Voice* or the *Native*, shoved their coins and bills through the narrow hole in the window and rushed on in their habitual hurry to get somewhere else.

Barrabas squeezed past customers coming through the door and stood in the narrow aisle that ran the length of the little store. The wall behind him was covered from floor to ceiling with magazines and comic books. In front, there was a counter over an ice-cream cooler, and glass cases filled with chocolate bars and Canadian cigarettes.

"Chocolate malt?" the woman behind the counter repeated to a tall man whose ear was rimmed with hoops and a diamond stud.

"Yeah, and can you do it with some extra syrup?"

"Sure," she said, leaning deep into the freezer and dishing scoops of chocolate ice cream into a paper container. Her oval face had gentle features, despite the severity of her long dark hair, which was pulled back in a tight ponytail. There was a no-nonsense quality to the deft movements of her hands, her dark brown eyes and quick smile.

She straightened to pour milk into the container and caught Barrabas's eyes with a startled gasp. She put her hand to her breasts, signaling surprise, and her face lit up with a smile. Barrabas felt a flood of happiness rising to his face. He smiled back. She shoved the container under the shaker, shoveled several spoonfuls of malt into it and threw the white-haired warrior a wink.

"Have a Nice Day Somewhere Else?" Barrabas read the words from the pin that held her waist-length blue cardigan together at the neck. "What kind of a message is that to give people, Anna?" he teased.

"Oh, I don't mean not to have a nice day here. I mean you to have a nice day somewhere else, too!" she answered, her English revealing the accent of her native Poland. She grabbed the milk-shake container, fitted a plastic top on it and took the customer's dollar.

"Best in New York, I swear to God," the man said, impaling the lid with a straw and walking out.

"And what can I do for you, Nile." She leaned slowly across the counter, closing her eyes and pouting her lips. He kissed her.

"How 'bout a date?"

"You know, I think I just finished for the day." She turned to the back of the shop. "Joe!" she yelled.

An older balding man emerged from a storeroom behind a curtain. A young, round-faced man stood behind him, meeting Barrabas's eyes and nodding slightly in greeting. A rapid exchange in Polish between Anna and Joe followed. They seemed to argue. Finally Joe put his hands up in resignation. "I take over, now. You go!" he told them.

Anna ran eagerly down the counter, tearing off her apron and grabbing a wool coat.

Anna Kulikowski had been one of the lucky ones. She had been active in the Polish women's movement, an adjunct of the workers' union, Solidarity. In 1981, she was visiting elderly relatives in New York when General Jaruzelski declared martial law and set out to eliminate Solidarity. She would have been interned if she had been in Poland. Instead, she took her place in New York's Polish community, scooping ice cream on Avenue A and writing articles on women's affairs for the Polish weekly.

They had met barely a month ago, over the counter at the newspaper stand. Barrabas had been instantly captivated. She was about thirty years old, and the few stray laugh lines at her eyes gave her an air of smarts that might have been missing in a younger woman. And there was a quality of strength and determination about her that intrigued him. It wasn't until a few weeks later that he had found out about her work in the Polish underground.

"Joe, he wanted me to work because he has his Solidarity friends over tonight. My brother, John, and Billy, Stanislav and their friends," she told Barrabas when they stepped outside.

The mercenary looked concerned. "I don't want to create difficulties for—"

Anna snorted. "Ach. They talk politics they read in the Polish newspaper all week, then they play poker and drink vodka until the sun rises. Come. What are we doing tonight?"

"How does two tickets to a Philip Glass concert at Lincoln Center and dinner for two at Raoul's sound?"

"Mmm." She leaned over and nuzzled her face against his neck. "Is very chic, yes?"

"Stick with me, baby." Barrabas grinned.

She slipped her hand around Barrabas's arm, and the two of them were off into the New York night.

Some hours later, they left a taxi outside Anna's apartment building on Second Avenue. She poked through her handbag for the key.

"We could still go to my room at the Plaza," Barrabas suggested again.

Anna shook her head. "You never tell why you live in hotels all the time—why you have no house to go to. So I like to make you come here. Everyone needs to have a little home somewhere."

They ascended the long narrow stairs in the old tenement building and passed down the bilious green corridors to a fifth-floor apartment. Anna undid three more locks, and they entered her apartment, a typical three-room walk-up, with a bathtub prominent in the kitchen. Barrabas walked to the living room and opened the metal grate that covered the fire-escape window. In the distance, the lights at the top of the World Trade Center sparkled. Anna approached from behind and handed him a glass of brandy.

"Can you sleep with me late tomorrow? I don't work at the shop until one."

The warrior shook his head. "I have to see someone. Early in the morning." He gestured toward the twin towers of the World Trade Center. "Over there, actually."

A slight pout came to Anna's full lips. She set down her glass, reached behind her head and undid the clasp that held her hair in place. The long silky brown hair flooded down her back and over her shoulders, rippling with a gentle curl in the city light that poured through the window.

"You never tell me what your business is, Nile. But even though I will never ask, someday you will have to."

"I know that." He almost turned away from her but resisted the impulse. What could he say to her or to anyone who didn't already know? That he was a professional soldier, and that he fought the wars he was hired for, signing up on the auction block with the highest bidder? His expertise was in destruction, and his skill was in killing. And there was his concern for Anna's safety. Knowledge could be dangerous at the best of times. Knowing about him could be deadly for her.

"I trust you, Anna, but—"

She put her fingers to his lips, closing them. "I will never ask. But you know."

Barrabas nodded. He did. If there was to be any kind of future for them, he would have to tell her. Without trust between two people, there was nothing. And trust was more than words. It was surrender. He was a warrior. How could he ever do that?

Anna lowered her head and sipped the brandy. She stood beside him, leaning her head against his shoulder. He felt the silky movement of her hair through the thin fabric of his shirt.

"Tonight, you have something on your mind. I see you at the concert: you did not hear any of the music. And when we go to eat, you do not touch your food. You talk to me all night, but I see in your eyes that you think about something else."

Oh, God, Barrabas thought. It's happening again, what happened to me and Erika. And it's my fault, not hers.

He turned to Anna, closing his big hands over her slender shoulders, pulling her to him. His hand slid down her back, pressing her body against his, and their lips met, their tongues battling in each other's mouths as they joined together.

He carried her to the bed, then slowly removed her clothing, kissing her eyes, her lips. Her body arched with pleasure when his tongue teased an earlobe, then curled down her neck. His big hands traveled across her body, massaging the soft mounds of her ample breasts, his fingers lightly squeezing her nipples until they hardened.

She moaned softly, slowly, with luxuriant pleasure. His hand encountered the soft fuzz between her thighs, and his fingers felt the slippery, inviting warmth. His mouth closed around her taut nipple, and he tugged it delicately between his teeth.

A groan of pleasure caught in her throat, and she writhed beneath him, spreading her legs to encompass his body. Her hands swept across his back, gripped his buttocks and continued their journey, feeling the immense hardness of his warrior body. Frantically she stripped away his layers of clothing, rocking urgently against him.

He entered her as an inarticulate murmur of ecstasy escaped his lips. Raising himself up on his hands, he gazed down into her eyes. She stared up at him, open and vulnerable, tentative yet offering everything. The soft rhythmic motions of joined bodies began, slowly at first, then building gradually until Anna gasped for air between her rising moans.

Their passion rose to an ecstatic peak where arms, legs, lips and tongues embraced, and the boundaries of the flesh dissolved in a climax that was timeless. They collapsed finally, their sweating bodies twisted and contorted upon the rumpled bed.

"Anna," Barrabas whispered between deep breaths, brushing his lips across her face.

She stayed awake long after he fell asleep, but he was oblivious to her fingertips exploring the contours of the scars that marked the story of his battles on his flesh. She knew already that he had gone away. She had seen it in the men she had loved in Poland, knew the signs of struggle, inner and outer, when men encountered missions and had no choice. She wondered if he would return, and when. She wondered if she wanted him to.

HE DREAMED. It was Saigon, the day he had been summoned to a joint meeting of the Military Assistance Command brass and representatives of the CIA, including an agent named Walker Jessup. After submitting his report on the mysterious intelligence material seized by the Fifth Airborne, Barrabas had recommended an extraordinarily dangerous course of action—that a small, select, highly skilled covert-action team of Special Forces soldiers infiltrate the headquarters of a North Vietnamese general named Chan Minh Chung. He had volunteered to lead it.

Desperately, he hoped the plan would be approved. It was probably his last chance to get back into the action before the war ended. And the success or failure of the proposed mission would likely determine the outcome of the terrible war.

The army driver eased the car through the front gates of the U.S. embassy compound and slowed to halt outside a wide door set in the small two-story building at the western edge. It housed MAC headquarters. Barrabas stepped from the car. Something told him he was dreaming, but he was aware of the thick air, the oppressive heat, the rays of the Asian sun beating down through layers of humidity. It was too real to be a dream.

He stood before the thick wood door, but before he could reach out to turn the handle, it swung inward. He stepped forward. But suddenly, as frequently happens in dreams, the setting changed abruptly.

He was walking across an arid field, yellow dust torn from the ground by the whipping rotors of choppers. In front of him, men carried the bodies of young men, the uniforms bloody and blackened. They slung them like logs into a pyramid of dead, where their mouths hung and accusatory eyes faced the sky.

Then he was aboard the helicopter, rising above the earth on a cushion of air; below, tiny men in black pajamas swarmed like ants over the landscape as far as the eye could see....

Suddenly back at MAC headquarters, he heard the door slam shut behind him with the ominous hollow sound of a drum. For a moment he was baffled. These were not the cool, dim, utilitarian corridors of the embassy intelligence command. It was the throne room of a marble palace, its polished stone walls as high as a Gothic cathedral. Far, far away, at the end of the long chamber, was a desk, tiny in the distance. A little man in a general's uniform sat at the desk.

In front of the general was a stack of papers and two enormous rubber stamps. He lifted one and stamped the top sheet of paper. It made a deafening boom that reverberated through the room. He slipped the paper to a stack on one side, with deft bureaucratic motions. The man lifted the second stamp and struck another paper. Another loud, ominous boom echoed like a drumbeat. He did not look at his visitor.

Intrigued and troubled, Barrabas advanced, the heels of his boots clicking on the hard marble floor in even counterpoint to the thunderous boom of the rubber stamps. As he got closer, he saw that the desk was huge, and he could make out the words written on the sides of the enormous stamps. One read Life. The other, Death. The pile of papers stamped with the second word was almost a foot high, the other pile scant inches, and still the man in the general's uniform pounded the stamps down faster and faster.

Then he looked up at Barrabas.

It was General Guetz.

He recognized the warrior. The stamps dropped from his hands. There was a wind in the room, swirling down from the high ceiling, snatching the papers from the desk and whipping them into a maelstrom of confusion, like fallen autumn leaves. The general started laughing. He leaned back in his chair, his hands gripping his sides, threw his head back and roared.

Something tugged at Barrabas's feet. He looked down. He was ankle-deep in thick red blood that gushed from the corners of the walls like jets in a whirlpool. The general laughed.

Amid the horror, Barrabas felt a sense of danger, of palpable evil more acute than in any of the numerous battles he had fought. He wanted to kill this man. In the way that dreams have of forcing conviction, he knew that if he didn't, he would die. The blood had risen to his knees and lapped halfway up the sides of the immense wooden desk.

Miraculously, a rifle appeared in Barrabas's hands. It was an M-16. He grasped it firmly, aiming at the laughing general. He squeezed the trigger. Bullets pumped from the barrel, tiny red-hot rockets, ripping across the general's chest. The man stopped laughing. His mouth set in a cruel line, and he glared with red eyes at the lone warrior. His beribboned uniform bore no trace of the bullets.

Again Barrabas aimed the M-16 at the general, but when he squeezed the trigger, his finger seemed to bend the metal. He looked at the gun. It was melting in his hands, dripping like toffee from his fingers. The blood had risen to his waist, flowing over the desk. Suddenly Barrabas felt gripped by an inexorable slowness. He couldn't move. He tried to step for-

ward, pushing against an immense invisible weight
that pressed against him.

The wind rose again, screaming and whirling
around his head, whipping the blood into frothy waves
that slapped against him. He tried to drop the disintegrating weapon, but it clung to his hands like Silly
Putty. The macabre general began to laugh again,
throwing his head back and roaring so loud his mouth
grew into an enormous red rictus. A wave of blood
washed over him, and he vanished.

The blood had risen to Barrabas's neck, and there
was the bitter taste of bile in his mouth. He tried to
reach over his head, grabbing at air to pull himself
from the gruesome whirlpool, but his feet remained
stuck, frozen in place as the level of the liquid reached
his nostrils. He sucked back a last chestful of air, and
then he was falling, dissolving into redness, forget-
ting who he was. He heard whispers, inarticulate but
soft, and was aware of warmth around him. The light
changed from red to whitish yellow, and like heat
flooding into a cold room, he felt relief. The feeling
that had gripped him in the general's room was gone.
He remembered it. An immensity of evil. He had escaped, but barely. Mercifully, his tormented aware-
ness ebbed, and he tumbled into deep comforting
sleep.

BARRABAS AWOKE to sunlight, the smell of frying
kielbasa and coffee. A TV in the kitchen was blaring
the morning news.

"Twelve bodies have been recovered from the spec-
tacular explosion that lit up the New Jersey water-

front yesterday, and police say there may be more in the ruins of the massive warehouse complex—"

He jumped from the bed, stepped into the kitchen and turned the TV off. Anna turned around from the stove where Polish sausage and eggs sizzled in a frying pan.

"In New York is always a disaster," she said whimsically. "They show a film of all these crowds of people downtown who watch the explosion yesterday. Just like the fireworks for the Statue of Liberty."

There was something about Barrabas's face that made her stop. She put down the spatula and kissed him.

"You sleep good?"

"Beautifully." He kissed her back.

She turned to the stove again and began flipping the eggs. "Easy over, you like them, yes? But I don't think you dream so good."

"Why do you—"

"You make sounds when you sleep last night. Like you are frightened, or feeling great pain."

"I don't recall." He slipped his arms around her slender waist. Smiling, she pushed him away and busied herself at the stove. She lifted the kielbasa onto a paper towel to drain the grease, turned off the burner and faced him again.

"When I hold you tighter, it was better, I think. So. I know you have business today. But first, I make your bath ready."

She pointed to the half-filled porcelain tub that ran along the wall next to the kitchen sink. Vapors floated on the surface of the hot water. "Watch your head."

She winked, pointing to the cupboard on the wall several feet above the tub.

"After, you eat breakfast with me," Anna added, her face clouding. She turned away from him, pretending to busy herself by lighting the oven, and putting the sausage and eggs in to keep warm. "And then you go."

6

A late autumn wind, cold and indifferent, swirled leaves and paper debris across the plaza of the World Trade Center. The twin towers soared overhead like giant dominoes a hundred and ten stories high. Around the base, three-story Gothic windows created the illusion of weightlessness, as if the massive skyscrapers floated over the granite plaza on a cushion of air.

Nile Barrabas entered the white marble concourse and descended the escalator to islands of elevators in a sea of purple carpeting. Stainless-steel doors opened and shut, enclosing or emitting a steady stream of men and women wearing suits and clutching briefcases. The offices of the Liberty Tribune were halfway up the building, on the fifty-fourth floor. He found the right elevator and entered, jammed shoulder-to-shoulder with a horde of tight-lipped workers who looked as gray as the November weather. The cage ascended with barely a whisper of sound, the upward movement discernible only by the changing pressure against his eardrums. With perfect smoothness, it stopped and the doors opened. The mercenary stepped out alone, and the stainless-steel doors sealed shut behind him.

The elegantly appointed corridor was empty, save for the hushed breath of circulating air. At the end, a wide wood-grain door with immense brass handles bore, in large golden letters, the words Liberty Tribune. To one side, a small brass plaque listed a dozen political-action committees, each name a variation on the notions of freedom, democracy and the American way.

Barrabas pushed through and stood inside a plush reception area. A dark-haired woman with heavy makeup sat at a big white desk, pressing buttons on a suitcase-sized telephone console. She looked up and glanced quickly at the visitor, making an instant assessment of the tall white-haired man from his chinos and casual navy windbreaker. Behind her, double doors of brushed steel led to inner offices. Almost immediately, Barrabas noticed tiny black holes in the dark wood paneling just below the ceiling, evenly spaced along the back wall. Video surveillance, he assumed.

"May I help you?" she asked.

"I'm here to see Mr. Guetz."

The receptionist smiled ingratiatingly, her heavily mascaraed eyelashes fluttering.

"Oh? Do you have an appointment with the general?" she asked in tones of gracious condescension.

"My name is Barrabas. I've come from the Fixer. Tell him that."

The woman's expression changed, vacillating between indecision and annoyance. Her hand hovered over the telephone. There was something about this

man's voice—an air of authority, perhaps, or was it
threat—that told her to obey. She picked up the telephone and spoke, waited briefly in silence, nodded
and hung up. "The general will see you. His secretary
will be right out to show you in." She coughed lightly.
"You'll, er, have to leave your gun here."

Barrabas didn't respond. The receptionist cleared
her throat again.

"Our security detected the presence of a weapon,"
she informed him.

Wordlessly Barrabas reached inside his windbreaker and withdrew the Browning Hi-Power. He
placed it on the desk, silently thanking her for her
foolishness. The information about the Liberty Tribune's security system was potentially useful.

A few minutes later a stern, matronly woman led
Barrabas through the steel doors. A wide circular
staircase spiraled to an upper level. A glass partition
separated the retired general's luxurious office from
the foyer. Beyond, windows opened to a panoramic
view of Manhattan's towers, the skyscrapers of glass,
stone and steel that grew like rock crystals from the
most expensive piece of real estate in the world.

At one end, an open door revealed a boardroom
with a long polished wood table surrounded by bro-
cade-upholstered chairs. More floor-to-ceiling windows gave a view of Manhattan. At the other end of
the office, the president of the Liberty Tribune rose
from his chair and walked around his desk to greet the
white-haired warrior. There was a moment of déjà vu,
the tangible sensation that he had been here before,
and then his forgotten dream from the night before

came back, the image of the general in a blood-filled room flashing through Barrabas's mind like an echo from the past. That was the dream that Anna had meant. It was terrible.

Guetz wore a light gray suit, a white shirt and a dark blue tie with red diagonal stripes. The expensive, carefully tailored clothing did nothing to conceal his massive shoulders and barrel chest. For a man of sixty, he was fit.

"Mr. Barrabas. Delighted, delighted." Guetz began to extend his arm to shake hands but stopped when his guest made no reciprocal move. He studied the mercenary's face, momentarily puzzled. "Have we met before?"

Barrabas stared at him impassively, then blinked once.

The retired general appeared not to notice the cold reaction. He turned away, pacing slowly along the windows overlooking Manhattan.

"I was certain that Walker Jessup would be of help. However, in view of these...explosions yesterday, it looks like someone jumped the gun." He laughed jovially and stopped beside his desk. He placed his hands on it, fingers spread widely apart, and inclined his weight forward. His voice became suddenly stern.

"Nothing untoward seems to have come of it—at least not for the Liberty Tribune. You can tell Mr. Jessup that I shall consider the fifty-thousand-dollar deposit nonrefundable. And thank you very much."

Barrabas faced him, his legs apart, hands stuffed into the pockets of his windbreaker. "And what about lives? Those twelve bodies they've pulled out of the ruins and however many may be in there. Are those refundable, General Guetz?''

"Please." Guetz put up his hands. "I'm retired. A 'mister' will suffice. Now I don't know anything about those bodies, who they were or what they were doing there. All I'm concerned about is the role of one of my employees. And I'll be dealing with that this afternoon by giving him notice."

"I think you do know who those men were. And why they're dead." Barrabas walked slowly toward the retired general, his blue eyes piercing the man like javelins. "I think you're responsible."

Guetz stepped back, obviously disconcerted. "You're crazy!" he exclaimed. "But then you'd have to be, wouldn't you, to be the kind of heavy that works for someone as unscrupulous as Walker Jessup."

The former general quickly recovered his composure and stood his ground. A little smile began to play across his lips. "Isn't this moral posturing a little disingenuous for a man in your line of work?"

The lines on Barrabas's face tightened. "I do the kind of work I'm cut out for. There are fundamental human standards that even I refuse to breach."

"Like what?" Guetz sneered.

"Loyalty," Barrabas shot back.

"Don't you dare speak to me of loyalty! I've spent my entire life in service to this country. To our way of life."

"Not our way. Your way." Barrabas stepped in front of the retired general and brought his head within a few inches of the man's face. "There is justice in the universe, Guetz. You're going to pay for what you've done.''

The president of the Liberty Tribune stepped back, momentarily flustered by the verbal assault. He moved behind his desk, keeping his eyes carefully on the white-haired warrior who confronted him. His next words verged on sarcasm. ''I suggest you get the proof first, Mr. Barrabas. That, after all, is what democracy is about. Now I know who works for Walker Jessup. You're insane. A pipsqueak two-bit tyrant! Get out!''

Barrabas remained for a moment longer, his iron stare lingering briefly on the older man's angry face. Then he turned and stalked out.

Guetz was immobile until the warrior had left his office. He straightened slowly, sticking a finger into the tight starched collar of his white shirt and loosening the pressure on his neck. He hit a button on his intercom.

''Send Dale Switzer in,'' he ordered, then turned the intercom off. He sat waiting. A few seconds later a husky man in his mid-thirties entered the office. His hair was sandy brown, his face heavily marked by long thin scars.

''That man who just left here...'' Guetz began. ''That was him.''

''Everything's on video, sir,'' Switzer snapped quickly. ''And I have some men downstairs who'll keep him under surveillance.''

''Take him out,'' Guetz ordered. ''As soon as possible, before he starts blabbing around.''

Dale nodded curtly. "And the other matter? He's waiting in my office."

"Deke Howard? Also a liability, but possibly still useful. The board is meeting on Sunday. I don't want any fuck-ups. You understand?"

Switzer nodded. He understood the general totally.

AFTER DESCENDING from the fifty-fourth floor, Barrabas went into a rest-room cubicle in the shopping concourse beneath the World Trade Center to examine the Browning HP. The mag was intact, and the inner mechanisms untampered with. He holstered it. As he left the rest room, his reflection in the mirrors caught his eyes. His white hair framed a face that was war-hardened but still young. His hair was his most distinguishing feature, turning his eyes into shards of cold blue ice. What these eyes have seen, he thought. And the story I have never told.

Through some strange mechanism of the brain, the dream he had forgotten that morning at Anna's apartment was again clear in his mind, dredged up from obscure cerebral synapses by his visit to the general's offices. In the beginning, the dream had started the same as it had so many years before—until he opened the door onto the macabre marble chamber and entered a nightmare. Prodded by winds from the past, his thoughts drifted to that Saigon day....

MAC's top brass had sat like a panel of judges, copies of his report in front of them, their eyes carefully concealing their opinions as they questioned him.

"And what makes you think the North Vietnamese have access to American military plans?"

"For one thing, the accuracy of their charts of our positions. They're too detailed for NVA resources. Unless they have satellite technology."

"The Russians have satellite technology, and the Russians are their allies."

Barrabas nodded. "But there's also the writing scribbled alongside. It was obviously done under strenuous—perhaps even battlefield—conditions. My translators insist it's not normal Vietnamese. It's a literal translation of English. As if they hurriedly copied the information from English documents. And the detail is too incredible for it to be accidental."

"Possibly," one of the CIA agents snorted. "But it's not enough to go by in my books."

"Then what about the bomb at the Majestic Hotel that wiped out half the South Vietnamese high command and my aide, as well? Someone had to be on the inside to even know about that lunch."

And then the MAC and CIA brass had turned away to make their decision, doubt lingering in their baleful expressions. In the eyes of one man, he saw perhaps a glimmer of sympathy. One of the CIA agents was a stocky Texan whose appearance even then was softening, on the verge of going to flab.

Barrabas awaited their decision for what seemed like hours, yet barely twenty minutes later they filed back into the briefing room, once again sitting at the long table like a row of stern patriarchs.

"The mission is yours," he heard them say. The decision was so unexpected that the words riveted him.

"We'll arrange for a patrol boat to rendezvous with you at a position on the Kap Long River. Mr. Jessup

here—'' the speaker gestured toward the Texan
''—will be aboard. He is to be your only contact. Any
information or material you collect is to be given to no
one else. Is that absolutely clear?''

Barrabas inclined his head in understanding. All he
could think about was that he was going back, out of
Saigon, out of a desk job, into the field, into action,
to the eye of the storm—where he belonged.

''You realize, of course,'' one of them continued,
''that the odds of your returning alive are close to nil.''

Almost in a daze, the decorated young colonel
nodded. It was nothing he didn't already know.

That had been the beginning of a mission that still
had no ending. Fate twisted strangely. More than a
decade later, it led him to an explosion on the New
Jersey waterfront. The loose ends had been left un-
tied long enough. The lure was set. It was only a matter of time....

Nile Barrabas shot a challenging glance at his image in the mirror, then left the rest room to join the
frantic crowds of noon hour shoppers in the underground mall. Wide subterranean avenues lined with
store windows led past mountains of glittering mer-
chandise. A light board announced the rising Dow
Jones industrial averages with rolling numbers,
straight from the New York Stock Exchange to the
busy consumers.

He saw a row of telephones underneath it, next to a
mirrored square column. Huddling tightly inside the
phone module to cut off the noisy hubbub of the
lunchtime crowds, he pressed the digits of Walker
Jessup's private number.

It rang once. The yellow telephone on the credenza behind the Fixer's polished black quartz desk was reserved exclusively for his number-one operative to check in. Jessup reached out and snatched up the receiver.

"Nile?" Despite his experience of Barrabas's anger, the huge Texan's voice was eager.

"The one and only. Jessup, you got a pencil ready?"

"Shoot."

"Get on the blower. I want Nanos, Hatton, Bishop, Hayes, O'Toole and Billy Two, if you can find him. On the double. I want them in New York by tonight. Tomorrow morning at the latest. Beck's hiding out in Connecticut. I want him to start using his computers to find out everything there is to know about the Liberty Tribune—personnel, board of directors, contributors, membership and holdings. Especially holdings in the metropolitan New York area. Got it?"

Walker Jessup scribbled madly on the yellow notepad in front of him, but even in his haste, his mind was juggling the possibilities. What in hell's he after? he wondered silently. Considering the currently tenuous nature of their friendship, he didn't dare ask.

"Anything on that tugboat yet?"

The Fixer sighed heavily. "Nile, you know what tugboats look like? The same all over. I'm working on it. So far, all I know for sure is that they don't dock in Manhattan anymore. That narrows it down to New Jersey, Long Island, and anywhere along a hundred and fifty miles or so of the Hudson River from here to Albany. Know what I mean?"

"Needle in a haystack."

"Close, but no cigar. Anything else?"

"Yeah. I'm going to rent some office space. Get your checkbook ready."

"Nile, how do you plan on paying for all this?"

"Fifty thousand dollars, Walker. Nonrefundable."

At the other end of the line, Jessup's spirits sank. After yesterday's New Jersey debacle he had consoled himself with greater, richer dreams of an around-the-world tour of the planet's finest gastronomical delights. Suddenly it all went *poof*. "Got it," he croaked sadly. His stomach felt abruptly empty. And the money he had riding the stock market was still committed for another month. There was a click, and the line went dead.

At the World Trade Center shopping concourse, Barrabas lifted the phone again and keyed in Anna's number. She answered on the second ring. Her hello was strangely edged with caution.

"It's me, baby. I called to say hello. And tell you how great it was last night."

"It was so good for me, too, Nile. Where are you?" she asked sharply, suddenly curious.

In the reflection on the mirrored column next to him, Barrabas saw a break in the throng of shoppers. A black-haired man in a long trench coat stepped through, his hands in his pockets.

"Gotta go," Barrabas whispered urgently, slamming the receiver back down and reaching inside his jacket. He spun around, dropping and throwing himself from the telephone module across the polished floor. The man in the trench coat brought his hand out of his pocket. He held a silenced revolver. It sputtered with a muffled sound, like corn popping in a covered pan. The telephone exploded into a shower of plastic and metal bits.

Barrabas fired twice. The shoppers froze, as if for a second the world had stopped. Bloody holes appeared at chest level on the trench coat. The man jerked twice, leaned precipitously and fell. Another man ran forward from behind him, aiming his gun with both hands. Two more soft pops sounded. A woman screamed. Then someone else. Instantly the shopping center was transformed into bedlam.

Shoppers ran for cover or flattened themselves on the floor, piling on top of one another in their flight to escape the bullets. A plate glass window behind Barrabas shattered, shards of thick glass crashing to the hard floor like chunks of ice. A mannequin's head was suddenly obliterated, and the plaster doll tumbled slowly from its perch.

Barrabas aimed again and fired once.

The gunman's face suddenly sprouted a small red eye in the center of his forehead. Blood spouted out the back of his head like water gushing from a hose, spurting over the fleeing shoppers. The dead man wavered uncertainly for a moment before his legs collapsed beneath him.

A new chorus of wails rose as panic spread through the concourse. Farther down the underground avenues, people turned to look at the commotion only to find panic-stricken shoppers bulldozing against them in a mindless haste to escape.

Barrabas looked around quickly and spotted an overhead sign pointing to the subway entrance. Two security guards appeared at the far end of the passage. They drew their guns and began firing. The long wall of store windows broke in sequence, an avalanche of dangerous glass sliding into the passageway. Barrabas swung around and aimed to one side of the two men. He pumped several rounds into the floor, chipping the hard tile and sending the guards scurrying for cover. He raced across the concourse, leaping over the prostrate shoppers cowering on the floor with their arms wrapped around their heads.

A unruly mob clamored at the stairs to the subway, pushing and shoving in desperate attempts to reach safety. He threw himself into the crowd. Security guards and policemen burst around the corner of the Chase Manhattan Bank. With his elbows protruding sharply and his feet kicking, Barrabas battered his way savagely to the front of the frenzied crowd and leapt over the turnstile at the bottom of the stairs. A rumbling vibration of the concrete floor and a loud thundering from the platform below signaled the arrival of a train. He rushed to the downtown platform, taking the stairs four at a time.

An incongruous calm prevailed, the waiting commuters staring with uncertain curiosity at the frightened faces of the people pouring into the station. Some began edging along the crumbling tile walls toward the far end of the platform. The train had pulled into the uptown side of the station, separated from the downtown platform by the deep pit of electrified tracks and a wall of blackened steel girders.

The commotion at the top of the stairs grew louder.

"Police!" a deep commanding voice shouted. "Let us through! Police!"

Barrabas jumped into the pit, narrowly avoiding the electric cables that ran along the inner track. He leapt to the second track across the low concrete wall. The doors closed on the uptown train, and the long gray cars began to surge forward. He jumped between two cars, grabbing the metal chain that hung between them, swinging his legs high, his feet scrambling for a hold on the metal step outside the end doors.

The subway train quickly gained speed, entering the long, dark tunnel between stations. Barrabas held still for a minute, breathing carefully and checking his grip. Beneath him, the silver tracks slid by under the metal wheels. Deafening thunder pounded from the concrete walls of the tunnel. He stepped over the chains, one leg at a time, until he stood securely on the wobbling platform between the two cars. A black man stood on the other side of the door, staring in amazement through the window.

Barrabas tucked the Browning back inside his shoulder holster, opened the heavy door and stepped inside. He winked at the black man. The commuter shook his head slowly in amazement. Already the train was slowing as it approached the next station. The warrior stood by the door, watching the platform as the train slowed. There were no police in sight. Not yet. His mind hummed. He'd set the bait, all right. He was the lure. And Guetz had responded—with a declaration of total war.

"Man, you in some hurry to catch this here train," the commuter beside him observed in a friendly voice, interrupting his thoughts.

Barrabas shrugged matter-of-factly. "New York," was all he said, feigning boredom with his eyes half-closed.

ON THE FIFTY-FOURTH FLOOR of the World Trade Center, the leader of the Liberty Tribune stared out his windows at the panoramic view of Manhattan. In the distance, a barge moved slowly down the middle of the East River toward the ocean. As he followed its progress with his eyes, he considered the culmination of his own plans. He'd forwarded messages about the board meeting to the four other members. Everything was ready to be set into motion. Progress, he thought, then heard the door open behind him and turned. It was the man with the scarred face. The general listened with his hands clasped patiently behind his back.

"They missed him. All hell broke loose. But he got two of them. The third one was far away enough to melt back into the crowd. No one to answer questions. The target escaped into the subway. And the dead men can't be traced." Dale Switzer's voice was curiously monotone.

Guetz nodded.

"I thought your people were better trained."

"Best that there is. This guy's tough. He's good."

The retired general's craggy face was hard, his teeth clenched with concern. Yesterday, they'd missed by only a few moments. This time, they were foiled again, and barely lucky to get away with it.

"Bring in Deke Howard," he said. "I think we can use him now."

Switzer walked to the general's desk and plunged his hand into his pocket. He took out a minicassette and waved it in the air.

"The third man got away with this. A complete recording of the telephone calls he made downstairs. They used the parabolic scope on him before he hung up. He's told Jessup to call in reinforcements." Switzer dropped the cassette onto the general's desk.

"And something else that might be useful," Switzer said, the pleasure evident in his voice. "He called his girlfriend. We got her number."

THE ADDRESS JESSUP had given Barrabas the day before was a crumbling one-story garage set in a row of body shops on a midtown street that ran down to the Hudson River on Manhattan's West Side. Despite the early-afternoon hour, the ladies of the night were out in full force, tottering in six-inch heels past idling semitrailers, with cheap fur pieces swathed around their scantily clad bodies.

Several stopped to hoot at Barrabas, pirouetting to swing their butts in his direction when he left the cab. Ignoring them, he walked past the covered drive-in bays to a narrow blue door and rang the bell twice. Several moments later, a middle-aged man opened the door as far as the night chain allowed.

"Jessup sent me."

The man nodded and closed the door. Barrabas heard the sound of the chain being unlatched. The door opened again, this time wider, and Barrabas was ushered into a narrow vestibule. He noted that a second tightly closed door led farther into the building.

"Pat Lily," the man introduced himself. His face was lined and weathered, his dark curly hair thinning to gray, and he wore thick horn-rimmed glasses. A small, politely rounded paunch protruded from his striped T-shirt. They shook hands, then Lily pressed an intercom button in the wall. A thick brass lock emitted an electronic buzz. Barrabas heard the sporadic popping of rapid gunfire as he and Lily pushed through the second door.

They stood in a long narrow warehouse, with half the length of the building taken up by a shooting range. Half a dozen human-shaped targets were arrayed under electronic gadgetry at the farther end. Bull's-eyes were marked faintly on the heads and heart areas.

Three of the lanes were in use, one target shooter to a lane. They stood twenty-five yards from their targets, with a variety of automatic weapons on tables behind them. Two of the men cast quick, disinterested glances at the newcomers and turned back to their practice. From the closely clustered grouping of the bullet holes in the targets, Barrabas could tell they were good. The third man pressed a button in the control desk behind his firing position. The electronic gadgetry hummed, swinging the bullet-ridden target up and replacing it with a new one. It was a professional operation.

The front of the warehouse was taken up by a small lounge area and a little glass-enclosed office, but most of it was a workshop with long benches equipped with drilling tools, vises, presses, bits and other machinery necessary for the kind of customized weaponry Jessup's friend specialized in. The mercenary noted carefully the soundproofing baffles lining the walls and ceilings of the entire building.

"For the neighbors," Lily told him, seeing his wandering eyes. "They don't exactly allow this kind of operation in New York. And even if they did, who needs inspectors? We got too many cops who belong to our club to put us out of business. They kind of look the other way, you know."

The weapons expert led him into the work area, where hundreds of bits and pieces of guns were grouped in orderly rows along the tables.

"My man, Mr. Jessup, told me you might have a rush job in mind," he invited, seating himself in an old oak desk chair and leaning back with his hands folded behind his head.

Barrabas nodded. "Something in the way of a genuine machine pistol. Maybe a Czech Skorpion. It has to be small, concealable. And real accurate. For situations where there's a lot of, uh, background noise. Not too messy, either. But effective."

Pat Lily pursed his lips, furrowed his brow in apparent thought and examined the white-haired warrior with narrowed eyes. He'd been in the business a long time. He had a talent for guns. But it was brains and instinct that enabled him to survive. The man he was looking at definitely knew how to kill. He had spotted that the moment he opened the outer door. After listening to the specifications, Pat couldn't help wondering what kind of job Barrabas had in mind.

"There's a famous old dictum—ever hear it?" he asked casually. "If we outlaw guns, only outlaws will have guns."

"I heard it," Barrabas replied tersely.

Pat gave a slight nod. "Walker Jessup's recommendation is as good as gold around here."

"Good." The mercenary laughed. "Because he gets the bill."

Pat Lily sat forward, his skepticism over. "What are you using now?"

Barrabas reached inside his windbreaker and withdrew the Canadian-made Browning Hi-Power. He set it on the desk beside Lily.

"You like it?" the gun expert asked.

"It's been pretty much my favorite pistol since I...I've been professional. Range isn't the greatest, and nine-millimeter parabellum don't always stop the big guys unless you hit them in exactly the right place. But I don't have much of a problem with accuracy. And it's small, light, has good muzzle velocity, and the twenty-round mag comes in handy from time to time. I'm mainly concerned about recoil. With rapid firing in a crowded place..."

"Like New York City."

The mercenary hesitated, watching Pat's face. They were speaking in signals now. An exchange of trust.

"I don't usually get involved in urban operations," Barrabas said carefully. "I don't like unfortunate consequences for innocent people."

"I know what you mean," Lily said, lifting the Browning from the desk and bouncing it in his hand. He pulled out the magazine and examined the barrel.

"Nine millimeter's good in that kind of situation. Keeps the kill localized. Not too messy. People nearby won't get upset about dry-cleaning bills. I think I can help you. Let me show you something."

Lily led Barrabas to the work area and carefully opened the combination on an ancient cast-iron safe. He took out a strange-looking pistol with an extra handgrip rising from the stock and at right angles to the main grip.

"Little adaptation patented by a friend, Dick Gillum at Ordnance Research and Development Corporation in Chicago. It's a prototype called CHAMP, which stands for Controllable Hand-held Accurate Machine Pistol." He threw it to Barrabas.

The merc caught it deftly and examined the curious configuration for a few seconds. It clicked. He put one foot forward, shifted his weight to the front and extended the gun horizontally, its left side to the floor, and his right palm down. His left hand formed a fist around the extra handle.

"The extra handle stops it from recoiling to the left."

Pat Lily smiled, visibly pleased.

"You got it. And you control the rear recoil by leaning into that modified isosceles-triangle stance you do with your legs. You're good at this, aren't you? Been at it for a while."

Barrabas grinned modestly and handed the pistol back to Lily.

"A real natural, I can tell," the older man said good-naturedly. He rummaged among some tools on a nearby workbench and returned carrying several

Browning magazines. "Come on over to the gallery here and check it out."

He led Barrabas to the shooting gallery, and lowered a target at the thirty-foot range. He loaded the prototype and handed it to the merc.

Barrabas spread his legs apart, closed his hands in a T around the two grips, aimed and fired, leaning hard into the recoil. Smoke burst from the muzzle, and the gun spat a stream of empty shell casings out the bottom, but it didn't move. A moment later, twenty neat little holes pierced the center torso area of the target.

Pat Lily was smiling from ear to ear. He hit the control panel again. The electronic equipment in the rafters of the warehouse hummed, whisking the target out of sight and placing a new target seventy-five feet away at the end of the gallery. He handed Barrabas a second mag.

A moment later, bullet holes zigzagged neatly up and down the target.

"I like it," Barrabas nodded, obviously pleased. "I like it a lot. It ejects the shells down in this position, too. Keeps them out of the way."

"No shiny little bits of brass to catch anyone's eye," Pat agreed.

"How many can you get for me?"

"None."

Barrabas was taken aback.

Lily put his hands palm up. "The CHAMP is a prototype. Not many around. But I can do something for you. Come here."

He led the way back to the work area and once again rummaged through piles of semiassembled, half-modified weaponry that were strewn across the work-benches. Finally he found what he was looking for. It was a Browning HP, identical to Barrabas's, with an extra grip attached to the stock in the manner of the CHAMP prototype.

"It's how the prototype was developed. I can get hold of some Brownings and modify them. Add the extra grips, and with a few minor—and illegal, I might add—adjustments, turn them into automatics. You won't notice the difference from what you've just fired. Besides, you're already familiar with the Browning, its weight, recoil. And I got the feeling you're pressed for time."

Barrabas took the modified Browning and tested it for its grip. It felt good.

"I need seven." He handed the pistol back to Lily.

"How soon?"

"Tomorrow. Morning."

The gun expert whistled softly between his teeth. "I'll have to bring in extra help for that. Work all night. We call that overtime around here."

The mercenary reached into his breast pocket and withdrew a small sheet of paper. "Here's a few other items I need."

Lily took it and scanned the list of matériel. "You're not kidding around, are you. It'll cost. A helluva lot. Especially on such short notice."

"Money's not a problem," Barrabas told him. "The Fixer will be more than happy to foot the bill."

7

"How much?" Jessup wailed on the verge of hysteria. "Twenty-seven thousand dollars!" Big round tears gathered at the corners of his eyes, and his fleshy face turned bright red.

"Shove it, Walker. You got us into this."

The elevator door opened, and Barrabas walked out, leaving the fat Texan in shock, holding his checkbook limply in one hand.

The real-estate agent was waiting for them in the corridor on the fiftieth floor of the downtown office building on Liberty Square. She was a thin, almost emaciated woman with too much lipstick and not enough eyeliner.

With one hand, she clutched a black briefcase tightly against her camel-hair coat as she strode ahead of the two men. The other hand moved in the air as she spoke. Both were covered with electroplated jewelry and synthetic gemstones.

"Such a hurry you two are in. You know, I don't usually make last-minute appointments like this on Friday afternoons— Do you have any idea what the traffic on the Long Island Expressway is like?" she bitched in a long, incessant stream of words.

They stopped by a veneer door, where a faded sign had once marked the proud name of the office space's previous lessees. She fumbled with a heavy ring of keys, finding the right one after a dozen attempts. The door swung open on ten thousand empty square feet of worn and faded carpeting, studded with protruding electrical fixtures. Barrabas and Jessup walked into the room.

"It's a lovely space, and very economical," the agent droned on in nasal tones. "Only a hundred and ten thousand dollars a month, quite a good deal, really. Electrical fixtures and computer hookups are already here, installed by the previous tenants, the accounting department of a large investment firm. What did you say your firm does?" She looked cockeyed at the tall man and the fat man.

"Uh, consulting," Jessup said quickly.

"Oh." She seemed satisfied. Then, her brows knit, she added, "What kind of consulting?"

"Uh." Jessup looked at Barrabas for help.

"We carry out surveys and research projects for a number of major international corporations."

"Oh." She nodded agreeably. "What kind of surveys?" she persisted.

"Uh—" Jessup froze again, and stammered nervously.

"Mainly in the area of transportation coefficients in relation to maximum intensities in the consumer profiles of large labor pools for heavy industry. It's a complex field." Barrabas had made it up as he went along.

The real-estate agent nodded slowly, obviously perplexed but apparently satisfied. "I see."

She marched farther into the empty office space, her hand waving again in midair. "Now, you notice that the Hudson River views are among the best in New York, and of course the rent includes..."

Barrabas ignored her, walking to the windows on the western side of the office tower. The late November afternoon was turning dark, and the lights in adjacent skyscrapers were on, revealing workers toiling at desks under acres of fluorescent lighting. It wasn't the view of the Hudson River that interested him. It was the view of the World Trade Center. The fifty-fourth floor. The offices of the Liberty Tribune.

He spun around and interrupted the real-estate agent's babble.

"We'll take it."

"What?" The woman seemed genuinely surprised.

"I said we'll take it."

"You realize there's a minimum five-year lease?"

Barrabas nodded. "We'd like to bring our architects in this weekend. To look it over."

The agent was taken aback. "Well, that's a little hasty, but I—"

"Can you arrange it?"

"Well, certainly. Of course, there'll have to be a deposit, say, ten thousand dollars?"

"Pay her," Barrabas ordered Jessup.

The Fixer gasped. "Ten thou—"

"I said pay her."

Sulking with anger, the Fixer pulled out his checkbook and put it against the wall, mentally muttering savage epithets about his chief operative who had suddenly become a tyrant.

What in hell had gotten into Barrabas, Jessup wondered. The mercenary wouldn't even say what he was up to. Pay this, pay that, Jessup bickered to himself. Twenty-seven thousand dollars for guns and ammo and a goddamn rocket. Ten for this. They still had to find a chopper. Nate Beck, the team's computer wizard, was on his way down from his Connecticut hideout with an order for five thousand dollars' worth of computer rentals. Kiss the general's fifty-thousand-dollar retainer goodbye, he thought, along with the much-anticipated Bermuda holiday, the round-the-world gastronomic tour, the sweet delicious flavor of—

Jessup was salivating. He scribbled his signature and handed the check to the stunned real-estate agent, positive that he could smell the unmistakable aroma of La Guanillo's chocolate chicken in the room. Jessup sighed. He wished he could control his deadly olfactory nerves. And he cursed all the unavailable, unobtainable cash he had committed to a ten-day ride on the stock-market bull.

NILE BARRABAS stood outside the Bleeker Street pub, taking in the sorry sights of rock-and-roll heaven. For three blocks, from McDougal to LaGuardia, the street was lined with taverns blaring an undistinguished cacophony of moldy oldies from the late 1960s. The crisp November air was pungent with the odor of burning marijuana. Cars with New Jersey license plates clogged the street, and long-haired kids from

Long Island and Queens in T-shirts sporting the names of heavy-metal groups jammed the sidewalks. Manhattanites, possessive of their island, referred to them pejoratively as the bridge-and-tunnel set. Mainly they were just a nuisance.

There were still hippies here, the warrior realized with astonishment. A man with a massive graying beard and a beat-up acoustic guitar played bad Van Morrison to a couple of young girls with stringy blond hair and dirty faces. A block away a young man bravely belted out a Fleetwood Mac tune with a voice that a third of the time couldn't quite hit the right notes.

Barrabas took stock of the taverns and bars, resigning himself to searching each and every one of them to find his man. Just then, another sound filtered through the noise, an awesome primal growl, followed by the crash of wood and breaking glass. The door of a pub burst open, and two men in duffel coats fled, casting fearful backward glances over their shoulders. They disappeared quickly into the sidewalk jam. The search was over.

The door flew open again. Another man sailed horizontally through the air, his legs scrambling for solid ground. He looked as though he'd seen the devil. As he stumbled to his knees, jumped up and ran, another fearsome groan floated from the pub. Barrabas knew who it was. He'd caught a glimpse of a head of thick coppery hair just before the door had closed. He took up position outside the door. It was only a matter of waiting.

Inside the tavern, the disturbance was getting ugly. The regulars weren't pleased to see their buddies' unceremonious departures. The owner wasn't too happy about the broken furniture. Liam O'Toole, the big Irish-American ex-sergeant, pushed his sleeves up his muscular forearms and prepared to face the music.

There was a gantlet of ugly faces ranging along the fifteen feet separating O'Toole from the door, and he could see from their eyes that they wanted revenge. There were far too many of them for him to handle. There was only one way out of it. Persuasion. The old Br'er Rabbit trick.

"Come on, ya lily-livered cowards, where are yer balls!" he yelled at them. "I'll take ya all on at once, and I'll wreck the rest of the place doing it."

He picked up the remains of an electric guitar from the tiny stage to his left, and with a forceful one-handed blow, shattered it against a table. The strings popped with a whine.

"Get him out of here!" the panic-stricken bartender screamed from behind the safety of the long counter.

O'Toole dropped the broken remains and beckoned them toward him. What the hell. He was too drunk to get hurt. "So you don't like my poetry, ya no-good scum bags. I'll force-feed ya knuckle sandwich." He balled his hands into big bony fists. "C'mon, ya hippy wimps."

They started coming.

"Throw him out! Throw him out before he wrecks the place!" the bartender screamed.

"You'll never throw me out. I'll tear you apart, limb by limb, and I'll tear this place apart, wall by wall!"

"Please! For God's sake, get him out of here!" the bartender begged again.

Finally they rushed him, grabbing his arms, legs, wrapping their elbows around his neck and lifting him into the air. Someone ran to the door and held it open. Liam O'Toole felt himself carried across the room like a battering ram. It's working, he thought. Whatever you do, don't throw me in the briar patch. What a bunch of no minds, he thought. Fools. They were so stupid they disgusted him.

O'Toole's antagonists let go, hurling him through the open door like a torpedo. The screams and epithets that followed were about as harmful as paper darts. He put his hands out and swung the lower half of his body down in preparation for descent when he noticed he was about to land smack-dab on top of someone.

A tall white-haired man stood just outside the door, hands on hips. A bemused smile was plastered across his face. The two big men collided. Barrabas fell back, grabbing two handfuls of the jumble of arms and legs that represented his second in command.

"Howdy, Liam."

"Why, Colonel! T'is indeed a surprise." O'Toole flashed a row of friendly white teeth as he landed.

"Having a good time, Liam?"

"Just straightening a matter out with a disagreeable bunch of drinkers who can't hold their liquor, sir."

"Well, get back in there and make them understand."

It took a second for Barrabas's words to sink in. O'Toole's smile vanished. By then he found himself flying through the air once again, this time in the opposite direction. The big ugly faces inside the tavern were even uglier. Eager hands stretched to meet him.

Barrabas brushed his palms off and leaned against the side of the building, listening to the yells, the smack of fists, wood splintering, glass breaking, the hysterical voice of the bartender, and an assortment of groans, screams, yells, shrieks, curses and grunts. From time to time, someone fled through the door and sprinted up the street without a backward glance. A small festive crowd gathered outside the pub to observe.

Gradually the noise of battle ebbed to a few final thuds, a last tinkle of broken glass. Liam O'Toole emerged from the pub, weaving uncertainly and wiping his hands on his pants. He had one of the biggest purple bruises Barrabas had ever seen, and a thin trickle of blood curled down his chin.

O'Toole smiled. "Finished, sir."

"You're a persuasive fellow, Liam."

"Baah. They're a bunch of dummies. What's up?"

"I could use a few of your talents on a project I'm working on."

O'Toole's Irish eyes twinkled with enthusiasm. "Glad to be of assistance. Where 'bouts?"

"Hometown."

"The Bi-i-ig Apple!" O'Toole whooped.

Barrabas nodded. "It has got a real nasty worm in it."

WALKER JESSUP WAS SQUEEZED behind the wheel of the white Dodge van, with Barrabas in the seat beside him. They soared down Manhattan's East Side on Franklin Roosevelt Drive, bumping in and out of potholes and lurching from lane to lane to pass the Friday-night drivers who clogged the freeway. On their left, the lights of Brooklyn were reflected across the dark still waters of the East River. On their right the massive blocks of public housing stood shoulder to shoulder, monumental mountains of brown brick.

"The White House ordered a one-third reduction in the staff at the Russian delegation to the United Nations," the Fixer explained. "Everyone knew they were mostly KGB. So the Company suddenly had a surplus of these mobile tracking units—MTUs."

"There are a couple of dozen mothballed in Queens. It was easy to get one. Traded a little favor for everything you ordered."

The back of the van was filled with a hundred thousand dollars' worth of communications and tracking equipment, including radar, sonar and infrared sensory devices. On the dashboard in front of Barrabas were myriad lights, buttons and dials, half of which he had no idea how to use.

The technology of surveillance was tenfold more sophisticated than it had been a decade earlier during his stint in military intelligence. That's why he had an expert on the team. Nate Beck, an electronics genius who had helped the military develop some of its first applications for microchip technology, was working with O'Toole, setting up a central communications headquarters in the newly rented office space.

Dr. Lee Hatton, the SOBs' female warrior, as well as the team's medic, had also spent time in most of Washington's secret agencies and knew how to handle the complex equipment. She was arriving in New York in less than twelve hours.

They passed under the huge stone arches of the Manhattan Bridge, and then the Brooklyn Bridge, the cables strung with lights, electric cobwebs delicately spun across the waters of the East River. Lower Manhattan, thick with clusters of monumental skyscrapers, spread to the west. It seemed almost implausible that the island did not sink under their collective weight.

"You said you managed to get some info on what was in that warehouse in New Jersey," Barrabas prompted.

The Fixer nodded. "Company source. Iranian military ordnance and spare parts. Bought and paid for by the shah before the Ayatollah took over. Mostly high-impact explosive material in that particular warehouse. Not as high impact as it used to be, because it's been sitting there for the past eight years and decomposing. Which makes it even more volatile. Those guys on the tug could blow themselves to bits just by dropping a crate."

"You tell your friends in the Company what we saw?"

A pained expression crossed the Fixer's face. "I...I had to, Nile." He glanced at Barrabas. The merc looked annoyed.

"It was the favor I traded."

Fighting anger, Barrabas said nothing. His silence was chilling. Anger came too damn easy to him these days. He didn't like it any more than Jessup did.

"Well, Christ almighty, you asked for an MTU, a chopper, a speedboat." The Fixer's voice rose higher. "How in hell did you expect me to get them on this kind of notice? Please, CIA, pretty please, with sugar icing on top?"

"As long as we're not tripping over half the federal agents in this country in the next few days..." Barrabas said lowly, sensing Jessup's frustration. He wanted the field clear, but the Fixer was right. There had to be a trade-off.

"Nile?" Jessup spoke softly. "I sure as hell wish you'd tell me what's going on."

Barrabas rode in silence for a few minutes. A debate raged within him. He wanted to tell Jessup everything—just to get it off his chest, if for nothing else. But he wasn't sure where to begin.

"I thought we're after whoever it was who was on that tugboat in New Jersey. I've been working on it for twenty-four hours. Nate Beck is using his computers to scan the Port Authority and Coast Guard records for the past week. I dunno," he sighed wearily.

Jessup glanced at the white-haired warrior. The blue lights of the city flickered over his face, periodically throwing into high relief the thin line of the shiny white scar that curved along his temple. Kap Long, Jessup thought. We go back a long way.

"I'm sorry I didn't fill you in yesterday. It'll never happen again, Nile. I promise."

"Forget it, Walker," Barrabas said gruffly.

The two men rode the elevated highway in silence again, approaching Battery Park, the tip of the island of Manhattan. The big ornate metal structure of the old ferry dock was a dark hulk against the glow from the harbor waters. Ancient piers jutted into the East River, abandoned for the most part by river traffic and transformed into parking lots.

The elevated freeway ended. Jessup turned the van around and headed back up the island underneath it. The downtown heliport was also situated on a converted pier, surrounded by a high wire fence, and brightly lit by mercury-arc lighting arrayed in rows on forty-foot pillars.

"What I don't understand is why you're setting up this whole operation with that fiftieth-floor space in the sky, this communications van, the chopper, bringing the team in when they're scattered over hell's half acre," Jessup persisted. "Until we get a line on the tug or some other break... Hell, Nile. It doesn't look to me like we're going in the right direction, and God only knows what those men who blew up the New Jersey warehouse are going to do next, sitting on a boat full of unstable explosives."

Barrabas reached across the seat and put his hand on Jessup's shoulder. "All in good time. I promise. Trust me."

Tight-lipped, Jessup braked in front of the heliport's security gate.

"Will you trust me?" Barrabas asked.

Jessup pondered for a moment. He nodded. "I trust you."

A security guard waved the van into the heliport, and Jessup drove to the end of the pier, to a sleek white helicopter with a red racing stripe painted along the fuselage.

"This is it," Jessup said, proud of his talent for appropriation.

"It's a beauty," Barrabas commented. The stretched cabin had two doors and an extra window on each side to give all seven passengers a full view. "It comes with the van?"

The Fixer nodded. "Fitted inside with matching surveillance equipment and preset scramblers for three-way communications between the van, the motorboat and Beck's situation on the fiftieth floor. It's a Bell 206L TexasRanger, disguised as a Long-Ranger."

"Looks like a limousine version of an army Kiowa."

Jessup laughed for the first time that evening. "There's no fooling the military eye, is there? The Kiowa is basically a 206A—shorter cabin with a longer rotor. Bell put out the civilian LongRanger, then adapted it for the military with upgraded engines, missile pods, roof sight, forward-looking infrared—or FLIR—and laser range finder. They called it the TexasRanger—after my home state, I might add. Now

the Company bought a TexasRanger, removed the
TOW pods, added the communications equipment
and painted it up to look like a civilian LongRanger.
Think Geoff Bishop will like it?"

"He'll love it," Barrabas agreed. "In fact I think he
flew one like it already. When we were down in Hon-
duras—"

He broke off, striding quickly to the edge of the
pier. Jessup shuddered. The man's behavior was getting more unpredictable by the minute. He trotted after the merc leader on short legs and came up beside
him.

"What's that over there, Walker?" Barrabas
pointed at an adjacent pier that jutted from the
shoreline a tenth of a mile away.

Jessup peered across the water. "A parking lot," he
replied with exasperation.

"On the other side."

The Fixer looked again. The unmistakable stack of
a tugboat was visible over the roofs of the cars.

"I thought you said tugs didn't tie up in Manhattan anymore."

"Well, I did, but—"

"I want it kept under constant surveillance until the
rest of the team gets here."

"You're going to watch it all night?" The Fixer had
a sudden sinking feeling in his stomach even before
Barrabas answered.

"Uh-uh. You are."

ON A SMOGGY DAY in Los Angeles, Harry Winston
returned late to his office after the usual two-martini

lunch and was disgruntled to find a telephone message waiting on his desk. He had planned on checking out and knocking off a few rounds of tennis before heading to his desert retreat for the weekend. What the hell, he thought, I own the company. Instead, he stood by the panoramic windows, deep in thought, observing the hazy yellow city sprawled beyond and below.

The movie business had been good to him.

Boom! Productions Incorporated was a Hollywood wunderkind, which had come out of nowhere barely three years earlier. Now they had thirty-two films in distribution, with six of them grossing forty to sixty million dollars worldwide. And climbing.

They hit a rapidly growing market at the right time, when the masses were yearning for muscular military heroes. Boom! had peaked with the release of *Nob One*, the true-to-life story of Navy fighter-helicopter pilots. But he knew that it couldn't last. The popularity of fake Soviet invasions had definitely waned since *Russians from Outer Space* almost failed at the box office. And there was only so much that could be done with the great Marine victory at Grenada.

True, Winston and his colleagues had done the job they set out to do. But the problem was evident. They were running out of wars. He had done the prudent thing, what any businessman with an eye to the future would do. He worked to ensure future supplies. It was a sound decision.

The phone number of his desk meant only one thing. They were going to move.

He punched a button on his telephone and heard the ringing at the other end of the line. He stood by the window, staring distractedly into midair. Someone picked up the phone.

"Winston."

Thousands of miles away, on the top floor of a Pittsburgh skyscraper, an industrialist leaned way back in his overstuffed swivel chair. Instead of palms, the view beyond his window offered columns of smoke belching from the forest of smokestacks that stretched, factory by factory, to the far horizon.

"I was just about to call again." The industrialist was a thin man with a slight mustache, and his voice possessed a secure quality, as lazy as a sunning cat's. "Did you see the article in *Isvestia* on your films?" He glanced at the magazine folded in his hand.

In Los Angeles, Winston snorted. "What are you talking about, Calvin? As if you read Russian any more than I do."

"I don't," the thin man replied, pulling himself closer to his immense marble desk and putting his feet up. "But since I do business with them, I do try to keep up. There's a journal that puts out monthly translations in English. It seems they've dubbed your phony war stories 'warnography.' Get it? To rhyme with 'pornography.' Clever, isn't it."

Harry Winston rolled his eyes and turned away from the window. "Yeah, right, I got it the first time. I didn't know the Russians were funny."

"Nor I."

"Well, let's call it 'warno' for short. I like that. Warno. Well, you gotta admit, we accomplished what we set out to do."

"You did," the Pittsburgh industrialist said, suddenly serious. "I hope you sold off your stock portfolio as I advised."

Winston shivered. It was really happening! He had kept twenty-five percent just in case Calvin was wrong. But if he lost it, so what. It was peanuts compared to what was ahead. His throat was dry.

"And I was just thinking about how badly Hollywood needs fresh material."

The man in Pittsburgh laughed. "Matériel!" he said, emphasizing the last syllable. As in weapons of destruction. And he made steel.

"We're moving?" queried the man in Los Angeles.

"Sunday morning. In New York. The final meeting. Nine o'clock."

THE REPRESENTATIVE from Virginia thrust his bony arm forward, index finger pointed accusingly at the witness who had been brought before the House committee.

"I suggest, Mr. del Fuego, that not only has there been widespread vote-rigging by the ruling party in your country, but further, that the Mexican government is riddled by graft and corruption!"

Whispers spread through the crowded room on Capitol Hill like wind rippling the water of a lake. The witness sputtered, his olive skin turning a reddish hue.

"That is all, Mr. Chairman." The representative turned to face the distinguished senator who headed the committee, bowed slightly and sat.

He shuffled the papers on the table, deliberately oblivious to his surroundings, "That should get us some headlines, sir," a voice at his elbow said. The politician turned to his young aide, beaming proudly, and cast a furtively concealed glance around the room. At the exit, the witness cringed past a gantlet of reporters and a volley of questions. The representative saw one of the network boys, and as their eyes met, winked and nodded almost imperceptibly. The interview was granted.

"By the way, this message came for you just a couple of minutes ago," his aide informed him.

The sheet of white paper had a phone number written on it. Then the time and date. Sunday, 9:00 a.m. He held it with both hands and stared, a little shocked. The noise of the committee room faded to a murmur. It was time. He turned back to the aide.

"Our Saudi friend, Prince Karo, is somewhere over the Atlantic on his way to London. Contact his people in New York. Give him this message. He'll know it's from me."

PRINCE KARO WAS ABOARD his private jet, thirty thousand feet over the North Atlantic, halfway to Europe from North America. He lounged comfortably, a plump man with a dark complexion, sorting through stacks of computer data on the low table in front of him. He had very nearly exhausted his entire inventory of weaponry and armaments with the completion of the recent shipments. And made a fortune. He was quite satisfied with it. The recent attempts at diversification had not been as successful as he had anticipated. And his life-style—villas and palaces in half a dozen major cities around the world—was expensive.

A small, slim man in a dark suit appeared at the door of the cabin, bearing a letter on a silver tray.

"It has been decoded, Your Highness."

"Set it here!" Prince Karo waved toward the table. The message had arrived from New York by radio transmission ten minutes earlier. The servant did as he was told and hastily withdrew.

The Saudi aristocrat could read the message from where he sat. He felt a thrill of excitement. Events were speeding to their final conclusion. He lifted a plump hand, heavy with jeweled rings, and pressed the intercom button in the arm of the sofa.

"Captain Khalid at your service, Your Highness."

"Captain, I've decided to return to New York. Immediately."

"But, Your Highness, we'll be flying into headwinds. Our fuel is—"

"Don't fool with me!" the Prince snapped. "Just turn it around and get me back."

8

Alex "the Greek" Nanos strode across the baggage area of the British Airways terminal at JFK airport, his white teeth contrasting sharply against deeply tanned skin and black hair.

"Hey, Colonel!" he shouted at the mercenary leader waiting patiently on the other side of the gate. "Great to see you." The Greek flashed a smile and slung his duffel bag over his left shoulder.

"Where's Claude?" Barrabas asked, shaking hands.

"Right behind—" Nanos looked over his shoulder. The black man was nowhere to be seen. "He was right—"

At that moment, a mass of mobile suitcases and diving bags stumbled through the gate, colliding with a matronly old woman and knocking an unaware businessman flying. Claude Hayes, a huge black man whose curly Afro-styled hair was tightly beaded at the back, lowered his arms. The piles of baggage dropped to the floor. He looked at the Greek with murder written in his eyes.

"Did we bring all that?" Nanos inquired innocently.

Hayes picked up a suitcase and nylon valise with a snorkel protruding from one end. "The rest is yours," he said flatly, stepping over the pile. "Good to see you, Colonel."

Among the three of them, they managed to get Alex's load through the busy terminal lobby. Barrabas had called them in from a sport diving expedition in the Caribbean. Nanos prattled on about it like an excited child.

"Bimini, Colonel. You ever hear of it? Little island near Bermuda, with a coral atoll. Great diving. Water's as clear as crystal. And there's these big stone walls underwater they discovered in '68. They don't know what in hell they're from, who built them or anything."

"It's really something, Colonel," Hayes added, obviously impressed by their experience. "A wall made of stone blocks that must weigh a couple of tons apiece. Completely underwater. I'd like to go back with some scientific equipment. Sonar devices, stuff like that."

"Yeah," Alex chimed in. "They say it's the ruins of Atlantis. It's spooky."

Hayes and Barrabas exchanged skeptical glances.

"It is spooky, though," the black man admitted.

As Barrabas's soldiers, both Nanos and Hayes had their main expertise in marine matters, Nanos as a navigator and Hayes in underwater demolitions. But while Claude Hayes had left behind a distinguished U.S. naval career with the SEALs, and fought beside his black brothers in two liberation wars on the African continent, Nanos had got the boot from the Coast

Guard for too many women and not enough subordination. They were as unalike as two men could be, but the missions they had fought in together had welded an unseamed bond between them.

"Whoooee!" Hayes whistled when he saw the communications equipment in the back of the van. "This for us? You gonna tell us what we're doing?"

"All in good time, Claude."

"Well, maybe you could hint. Like, what's the theater of operation?"

"New York City."

"Urban warfare?" Nanos was surprised. "Not our usual area of expertise."

"Man!" Hayes cried. "I grew up in the Detroit ghetto. I know urban warfare like I was born to it. The city is my stomping ground." He bristled with pride, and the beads in his hair shivered.

"Well, pitter-patter, let's get at 'er!" Nanos jumped enthusiastically into the back.

"One more stop," Barrabas told them. "American Airlines terminal. Lee and Geoff's plane should be landing in about ten minutes."

"What about the others?" Nanos asked. "O'Toole, Beck and that loony Osage Billy Two?"

"You'll see O'Toole and Beck in a few minutes. As for Billy Two, Jessup put out the call, but so far there's been no answer."

"He's been an unreliable son of a gun ever since the Russian GRU agents pumped liquid sulphur through his system," Hayes commented sadly.

"I'd say unpredictable more than unreliable," Barrabas noted.

"Silly Indian's probably out in the desert melting his eyeballs by meditating on the color of the sun," Nanos joked half-seriously.

"Well, he's always welcome aboard," Barrabas told them. "And he has a habit of turning up at the right place at the right time."

They drove around the highway loops that led among JFK's odd futuristic terminals.

"This place always reminded me of a spaceport on Mars," Hayes commented wryly.

Barrabas parked in front of the square facade with the familiar American Airlines logo. He and Hayes left Nanos behind to fend off the traffic cops and headed inside the terminal. The monitors registered the flight from Montreal under the arrival column. The two mercs took up a position on a balcony overlooking customs. Through the glass wall they looked down on the lines of newly arrived travelers queuing in front of the customs officers' booths.

"There they are," Hayes said, pointing to the farthest line. A man of medium height stood next to a slender woman with short-clipped brunet hair. "I can't get used to Geoff having blond hair."

"At least it matches his forged passport," Barrabas said quietly. "If the authorities didn't think he was dead, he'd be the object of one of the biggest manhunts in history."

"Man, he got a bum rap. The worst." Hayes folded his thick arms across his massive chest and shook his head sadly.

Geoff Bishop, a celebrated veteran flyer of the Canadian armed forces, had been recruited for the SOBs as a pilot. On a mission in Florida, he had single-handedly saved the governor of that state from a terrorist bomb. A press photographer flashed a picture, and in the confusion, Bishop was labeled as a terrorist. The mistake was compounded by the Canadian's subsequent disappearance. He was believed dead, made notorious by the media, his name listed in the annals of infamy as an attempted murderer. And there was little anyone could do to clear him.

That was the deal. Barrabas and the SOBs were unsung heroes, a covert action team that served the whims of the U.S. government on condition of total, absolute secrecy. Walker Jessup was their only connection to the powerful House committee that gave them their assignments. If they were to be caught or killed, if they were to be accused of being agents of American imperialism or whatever, no one in Washington would officially know anything about them. Suddenly they would become private operators, responsible for their own actions and their own failures.

And when they won—and they had always won—there was no praise, no monument, no glory. A few thousand bucks tucked away in a bank somewhere was their reward. That, and the satisfaction of knowing they had kicked ass and survived once again. It took a special kind of man—and woman—the kind that lived on the knife's edge between death and danger, risk and the odds against them. They were like addicts who needed a hit of action just to survive in a world that otherwise didn't have much place for them.

"At least he's still got Lee Hatton," Barrabas murmured. For a long time, Hatton and Bishop had kept their affair a secret. It was out in the open now, but both of them had made it clear that the subject was taboo for everyone when they were on assignment.

"They're good people," Hayes agreed. "They deserve each other. Yes, they do. You ever worry about them being together in battle? You know, distractions as lovers."

Barrabas grimaced and shook his head. "Nah. They're real professionals. Their relationship never interfered with the job at hand."

"Uh-uh."

"Hold it," Barrabas said sharply, his eyes riveted to the customs booths below. Lee Hatton had been cleared quickly, but the customs officer was lingering over Bishop's passport. Tension knotted in the bellies of both men. The officer snapped the passport shut and handed it back. Hayes heaved a sigh of relief.

Down below, Bishop and Hatton were gazing up at the window and waving at the two men. Hayes and Barrabas returned the signal. A few minutes later the two newly arrived mercs came out of customs.

"Any baggage to collect?" Barrabas inquired after exchanging greetings.

"No," Bishop told him. He pointed to the flight bags they carried. "That's all there is."

"Unlike our friend Nanos," Hayes commented dryly.

The Greek waved to them from the van as they came through the sliding doors.

"Hey, Bishop!" he called to the airman. "Is it true blondes have more fun?"

The Canadian laughed and winked as he climbed into the back of the van. "Damn betcha, Greek."

"That's why we took the later flight," Lee explained. "He had dark roots showing, so we had to do a quick dye job to match his passport."

"I tell you," Bishop commented, brushing his hand across the top of his head. "If I have to do this one more time, it's going to fall out. By the way, did you see the name Jessup put on this thing?" He thrust his passport in front of Barrabas, open to the photo.

"Johnny Manitoba?" the mercenary leader read incredulously.

Bishop nodded. "Yeah. He added my middle name to the name of the province where I was born. The customs officer did a double take. I tell you, 'John Doe' would attract less attention than this moniker."

"Yeah, but Geoff was great," Lee added, looking at Bishop with obvious admiration. "Told customs his grandfather was a deaf and dumb Ukrainian who could only write the name of the province he was going to when he emigrated to Canada in 1910."

Bishop laughed. "That part's true." He slammed the rear door, and Alex pulled the van into the traffic leading to the city.

"How do you feel about having to put up with this subterfuge every time you cross a border?" Barrabas asked in a serious tone.

Bishop heaved a deep sigh and thought for a moment. "It's getting easier," he said finally. "As long as I'm officially dead, I guess they're not looking for me. And let me tell you—it's good to be alive.''

"How are you at flying a TexasRanger?"

Bishop's face lit up like sunshine. "Mmm. Christmas has come a month early, Colonel. It's one of my favorite choppers. They have a ride smoother than a baby's bum.''

"Where to, Colonel?" Nanos asked, skimming through the freeway traffic. In the distance, Manhattan's towers rose above the endless rooftops.

"Follow the signs to the Brooklyn Bridge."

A short while later, the mercs crossed the East River under the soaring stone towers of the world's first suspension bridge. The Saturday-morning traffic was light, and the streets of the financial district were devoid of vehicles. Soon, the mercs were riding the elevator to the fiftieth floor of the skyscraper at Liberty Place.

The ten thousand square feet of office space overlooking Manhattan had been transformed overnight into an aerial fortress. The windows had been draped with one-way reflective plastic, allowing views out but not in. Carefully arrayed along the worn carpet on one side were the specially modified Browning HPs, cases of spare mags, a dozen Colt commandos—the shorter, close-quarter version of the M-16. But the gadget by the western window elicited exclamations of surprise from the mercs.

A chest-high tripod held a six-feet-long tube launcher, evidently aimed directly at the World Trade Center. Wires led to the electronic-signals generator and optical sensors in separate mobile cases. Nearby, three TOW missiles lay neatly together in five-feet long canisters. Liam O'Toole, busy with some final adjustments, didn't notice the mercs' arrival. Nate Beck waved to them from a long row of portable tables where computers, monitors, printers and modems clicked, whirred, ticked and blinked. Thick insulated electrical cords snaked along the floor, and a communications cable wound its way to the roof of the building through a hole drilled in the top of the fire exit.

"Colonel!" the computer wizard called. "Can we talk?"

Barrabas nodded. "Look around," he told the others. He pointed to a long table covered with maps. "We'll rendezvous right there in a few minutes."

The mercs sauntered across the room toward the launcher, shaking their heads in astonishment. O'Toole was oblivious to them until they were right behind him.

"This ought to punch a hole in real-estate values," Nanos cracked, patting the tripod.

O'Toole looked up from the optical sensor, smiling when he saw his buddies. "Yeah, I figure the colonel got tired of playing the stock market and decided to speculate in skyscrapers."

"He should be able to pick up a few bargains after playing around with this," Lee laughed.

"Are you kidding?" Hayes said. "Half the Lower East Side is bombed-out ruins, and they're still paying hundreds of dollars a square foot. In New York, they like to live that way."

"The colonel hasn't by any chance filled you in on what we're doing here, has he?" Bishop inquired of the Irishman.

O'Toole looked up from the wires and over his shoulder, spotting Barrabas talking to Nate Beck across the room. The redhead spoke in a near-whisper. "Whatever it is, it's eating away at him something crazy. Other than giving the orders to get this place set up, he hasn't had two words to say."

He pointed to a row of army cots that had been set up in one area. "Nate and I crashed out for a while last night. He kept going all night long, and he's no worse for the wear. It's like he's got a fire burning up inside of him, and the devil knows when it will burn itself out."

"What's all this?" Lee called, walking toward a bulky telescope on a tripod ten feet away. A light on the housing above the eyepiece blinked on and off, and a long cord led across the room to Beck's electronics-control area.

"Have a look," O'Toole invited.

A small section of the reflective screens had been cut away from the window in front of the telescope. Lee put her eye to the end. At first the focus seemed off, as if a gray filter had been attached to the lens. Then she saw a thin beam of red light streaming from the housing along the top of the tube. It ran for almost a quarter of a mile, inclining slightly until it hit a window on the fifty-fourth floor of the World Trade Center.

The other mercs joined. "Infrared sensor," one of them remarked.

Lee nodded. "An eavesdropping device. I remember a demonstration once, back when I was in intelligence in Washington. I never used one, though."

"You guys mind explaining to the dummies?" Alex pressed for an explanation, pointing at himself.

Lee straightened and motioned for him to have a look. "It throws an infrared beam against a window up to half a mile away and transfers sound vibrations back into an audio-sensor unit. You can listen to a conversation as if you were in the same room. The scope filters out other light spectrums and allows you to aim the beam, which is normally invisible to the naked eye. What's the colonel using this for?"

O'Toole shrugged. "He wants to know everything that goes on in that suite of offices over there. That's why he chose this office building to set up in. Nate's been monitoring the feedback. And so far there hasn't been any."

There was an awkward silence for a moment as each of them wondered what the colonel was up to.

"He said all in good time," Bishop reminded them. They exchanged knowing looks. They had trusted the mercenary leader with their lives too many times to count. They could trust his secrecy awhile longer.

Over by the computers, Barrabas was deep in conversation with Nate Beck.

"Colonel, one of the way these—PAGs—political action groups make money is by selling their mailing lists to commercial mail-order companies, publishing clearing houses, even religious direct-mail campaigns. With the computer, I traced a mailing list for one of the PAGs that shares space with the Liberty

Tribune to a mail-order Bible company in Ohio, tapped into the rest of their two-hundred-odd mailing lists and found one that originally belonged to the Liberty Tribune. Now the interesting thing is this—''

He tapped some instructions into the computer, and the screen blinked. A list of names appeared.

''There are tens of thousands of people on those lists, most of them Mr. and Mrs. Ordinary Schmoe in places like Break Neck Creek, Indiana. But several dozen names kept coming up. Using their addresses, I started searching local banks and state corporation registers.''

He pressed another key. The screen blinked again, and a short list of six names appeared. ''These six are filthy rich. What's even more interesting is that they own dozens of interlocking companies, sit on boards together. And two of them are registered founders of the Liberty Tribune.''

''Good work, Nate. Have you been able to connect any of them with the tugboat?''

''I'm working on it, but I still haven't found the missing link, and I've got the computer accessing corporate files everywhere from Delaware to Bermuda— corporate tax havens. I do have this, though.'' He handed Barrabas a sheet of paper. ''It's a list of all the property in Manhattan owned by the companies that are owned and controlled by the six names you see on the screen.''

Barrabas scanned the paper quickly. There was hundreds of millions of dollars' worth of real estate listed. ''Keep going, Nate. And find out everything you can about these people.'' He pointed to the screen.

"I want it all, right down to the names of their country clubs and their mistresses. Any activity across the street?"

"You mean via the infrared audio-sensor?" He shook his head. "Just the char ladies last night and a couple of security guards. It's the weekend; you figure someone will be there?"

"If they are, I want to know about it pronto."

He left Nate to continue his computer search and called the other mercs to join him at the map table, which had a large chart of Lower Manhattan tacked to its surface.

"First of all," he told them, "some background."

The explosion on the New Jersey waterfront had made the international news as far as Bermuda and Canada, but the mercs had paid little attention to it. Suddenly their leader was giving them an angle.

"You mean somewhere in New York a bunch of Central Americans are sitting around with a boatload of high-impact explosives?" Nanos asked.

"One thing I'm sure of is that there were no Central Americans involved. Before they started shooting, they were shouting orders, and it wasn't in Spanish. It could have been Farsi."

"Modern Persian," Hatton supplied. "So the Iranians got what they wanted by playing on the privatized war against Nicaragua and tricking this Deke Howard guy."

"Could be," Barrabas agreed. "The big question is what they're going to do with a tugboat full of decomposing, highly unstable explosives."

"Maybe they've transferred them to a freighter. They might be halfway to the Persian Gulf by now," Hayes suggested.

"It would hardly be worth the effort, for one thing. That many explosives would be worth diddlysquat in the war against the Iraqis," O'Toole pointed out.

"Right," Barrabas said. "But enough to do a lot of damage here in the Americas."

"And it might not even be an operation officially sponsored by the Iranian government," Lee Hatton added. "There are so many Shiite extremist groups in the Middle East. For instance, the Hezbollah—the Party of God. They've been vowing for years to bring terrorism to American soil."

"So what are all these pins stuck in the map, Colonel?" Claude Hayes asked.

"You've all seen the van. It's our mobile communications unit. Lee, Alex and Liam are in charge of it." Barrabas lifted a pointer from the table and indicated a white pin on the waterfront. "That's your chopper, Geoff. You get the bird's-eye view. By the way, you'll find it full of rappeling equipment. I've tried to take care of all contingencies. Manhattan is made up of two things—roads and roofs. If we have to launch an assault, we may find it easier to land on top of a building and work our way down rather than start at street level and go up."

He touched a third pin on a pier near the Staten Island Ferry Terminal. "Claude, I'm asking you to work alone for a while. That's a high-speed racing launch with a cabin to keep you warm, and communications equipment to keep you in touch with the rest of the team. I want you to be prepared for scuba work—including possible underwater demolition—at the drop of a hat.''

''Aye, aye, Captain.'' The black man saluted. ''The one thing missing is the tugboat. Have you got a line on that?''

Barrabas's pointer homed in on a red pin stuck in the East River. ''Pier eleven. I want it kept under steady surveillance. One of these days—hours—they're going to move.''

''How do you know they already haven't?'' Bishop asked.

''Because Walker Jessup has been keeping an eye out.'' Barrabas glanced at his watch. ''And he's into his twelfth hour. Let's get armed and dressed and get going.''

Just as the mercs started to move away, O'Toole jerked his thumb toward the tripod on the west side of the room. ''Colonel, does this have anything to do with the TOW missile aimed at the World trade Center?''

Barrabas hesitated. ''Like I said, Liam. I'm preparing for all contingencies.''

9

With their handguns carefully concealed beneath bulky windbreakers, the mercs used the service elevator. The white van was parked in a loading bay at the back of the office tower. Barrabas let Nanos take the wheel while he climbed into the passenger seat.

The sidewalks of Manhattan's financial district were relatively deserted, and the normally frantic vehicular traffic virtually absent. As Nanos wound through the narrow streets between towering canyons of high-rise buildings, Barrabas found his thoughts inexorably drawn to memories of the mission more than a decade earlier....

The huge base camp at Pho Doc sprawled over the slopes and valleys of three hills, buzzing with the activities of thousands of men at war. To the east, fighters and bombers landed in tandem on the strips that ran across the flat farmlands. To the north, a tent city housed thousands of newly arrived young men. Below him, in the first valley, was the hospital, with processions of ambulances carting the wounded in and the dead out. Farther to the south were long narrow portable buildings housing administration and recreation complexes.

The decorated officer surveyed it for a moment, knowing it might be his last time. The air overhead swarmed with approaching Medevac helicopters. A jeep wound its way along the trail that led up the side of the hill to the landing zone. "Colonel, that's the commander of the *Callisto*," a young man behind him said.

Barrabas turned and nodded. "This will just take a minute. Then we'll leave."

"Yes, sir!" The lieutenant saluted, smiling with anticipation. He ran toward the waiting chopper. Not far away, the first of the arriving helicopters hovered over the crest of the hill, its rotor swirling dry dusty earth and bits of straw into a maelstrom.

Barrabas had picked two of the Special Force's best, young men with stamina whose trained and hardened bodies were lethal weapons. They knew the risks involved in infiltrating Chan Minh Chung's camp. But risk was what they lived for.

The jeep stopped in front of Barrabas, and a lean man in camouflage fatigues jumped out. Deke Howard wore the insignia of the 17th Waterborne Assault Group on his breast pocket. He saluted Barrabas.

"Colonel, I hear you need the services of the *Callisto* again," the lieutenant said.

"I requested your patrol boat specifically, Deke."

"Didn't know you had it out for me, sir." Howard winked.

"I only have use for the best."

There was a moment of awkward silence. Despite Howard's friendliness, Barrabas knew the young lieutenant fought an instinctive dislike for him. The two officers had met when they worked together several years earlier in a run on a VC compound in the Mekong Delta. Today they made light of it, but they knew the mission ahead of them, deep into the delta of the Kap Long River, was a journey into the heart of terror.

"I leave tomorrow morning, and we rendezvous at the abandoned canal in three days." Howard repeated the arrangements. "My instructions are that I'll have a passenger, Walker Jessup, CIA. You know him?"

"Not much." Barrabas shook his head. "Just met him a few days ago. He came through with support for this mission when it was needed. Seems like a steady guy."

"Who's taking you in?"

Barrabas jerked his thumb toward the waiting chopper. "We go out with a platoon on standard hit-and-run reconnaissance and separate at the LZ. It means we hike overland for a day, but that way the VC won't see us coming."

"And how far is our rendezvous from, uh, wherever it is you're going?"

"Anywhere from a few hours to half a day, depending on the swamps we have to go through. Probably have a search party on our tail and be in a hell of a hurry."

"I'll keep the engines warm," Deke promised.

Barrabas noted a degree of concern in the lieutenant's expression. "Is there a problem?"

Howard screwed up his face. "Hasn't rained in a few weeks. Country's dry. It means the water levels will be down. It's a thirty-one-foot patrol boat. I just hope we don't have to shovel any sandbars out of the way, if you know what I mean. Could use some rain, that's all.''

Barrabas looked at the sky. It was deep blue, and the hot sun beat down. The monsoon season was late this year. "Maybe we'll get lucky," he commented, knowing that what was good for the *Callisto* would make his own overland journey an impossible hell.

"Well, that's it, Deke. I just wanted to run over things with you before I went. Last time, we worked well together. That VC ambush had the whole patrol pinned down, and you and I were the only ones with enough guts to outflank Charlie on each side and give them a taste of their own medicine."

Howard threw his fist into the air.

"Pincers of death!" he crowed over the rising noise of landing choppers. It was what they'd dubbed themselves in the exuberance of the victorious aftermath.

For a few brief seconds, the barrier between the two men dissolved. Barrabas laughed. "Well, let's hope once was enough."

"I second the motion. I'll see you in three days. I'd wish you good luck—" Deke looked at him strangely "—but you already got it." He returned to the jeep.

Barrabas watched it speed down the hillside, back to the main camp. He kicked at the dry powdery soil, reflecting on Howard's last comment. A lot of officers felt that way about Barrabas—a man, still young, who had risen steadily in the ranks and had earned a lot of respect. He had more decorations than he could count, and a reputation for heroism that made enlisted men eager to follow his command. Some fellow officers—the ones with small minds—were simply jealous and petty, sometimes even vindictive. Others assumed that Nile Barrabas, like themselves, had been born with a silver spoon, growing up accustomed to privilege and prestige.

Few knew the truth about the poor Wyoming rancher's son who ran away at seventeen to join the Army. It was evident that Deke Howard respected him. But like many others, the *Callisto*'s commander assumed things he had no right to assume. That life hadn't been a struggle for Nile Barrabas. Because everything the colonel had, he'd had to work for—or fight for.

A shout from the chopper brought him back from his thoughts. He turned and saw the rotors slowly turning. Not far away, the Medevacs were landing, and soldiers rushed to unload the wounded and the dead. Already, the corpses of young soldiers were stacked like firewood, high as a man's chest. Ambulances careered up the side of the hill.

The chopper rose and hovered a foot off the ground. It skimmed over the top of the high grass until it slowed in front of him. He ran to the open door, and two Special Forces lieutenants reached out to pull him in. Immediately the chopper rose above the earth, and the base grew smaller, until it looked like a fragile toy, tiny and far away. Colonel Barrabas brushed his hand through his chestnut-brown hair as the pilot turned south, heading toward the Mekong Delta and the encounter that would change his life forever....

Years later, in New York City, he was thousands of miles away from Vietnam, yet once again the age-old tale of hunter and quarry was about to play itself out to its inevitable conclusion.

WALKER JESSUP STRETCHED his neck by rolling his head slowly clockwise three hundred and sixty degrees. It didn't help. He'd been cramped behind the wheel of his BMW, parked underneath the elevated highway with a view of the tugboat—for days, he thought. He was bleary eyed, stiff, sore, fatigued, and his skin felt sticky from sweat. His left eyelid twitched, and the fifth vertebra up from his tailbone was in excruciating pain.

Worse, he felt fat. The steering wheel had put a permanent indentation in his bulbous stomach. The BMW's leather bucket seats were luxuriously comfortable, but not for sitting up straight twelve hours at a time. He hadn't done this kind of surveillance since his bird-dog days with the CIA three decades ago. He thanked the gods for one small mercy. The bullet-pocked windshield had been replaced.

He cursed Barrabas, and he cursed himself for allowing the colonel to guilt-trip him into doing this. Then he included the Iranians, the tugboat, General Guetz, the fifty thousand dollars, the temptation of chocolate chicken at La Guanillo, and all the dough he'd stupidly plowed into the stock market for a ten-day ride.

Twelve bloody hours, he thought, watching this damned boat all night long, and the only thing I've seen so far is two guys come out to smoke cigarettes.

There was a tap on the window. He looked over and saw Jimmy Ducett, his assistant, peering in. The young man waved a carry-out tray with breakfast. Jessup pushed a button that unlocked the doors. Ducett opened the door and sat in the front passenger seat.

"How's it going?" he asked, pushing the cardboard tray in Jessup's direction. "Jumbo coffee, triple cream no sugar, and a fried-egg sandwich on whole wheat." He sniffed at the air. "Whew. Stinks in here. You been here all night?"

Jessup ignored him and opened the waxed-paper wrapper. He peered at the mangled-looking mess on toast.

"I hope you like ketchup," Ducett chirped innocently. "I wasn't sure."

Jessup looked glumly at the sandwich. In the circumstances of feast or famine, it was, well, nourishment at least. He bit. He chomped.

"Not bad," he said between mouthfuls. "The ketchup kind of masks the flavor of the grease. Tell me, Jimmy. How can you dress like that first thing in the morning?"

Ducett's getup made it difficult to imagine him as a former corporal in the Airborne, Barrabas's old regiment. His hair was greased back along the sides and up in the middle in a mild Mohawk, and his black leather jacket was covered with silver studs. He wore a white T-shirt and tight-fitting blue jeans that barely reached down to the high black boots laced up to his ankles.

Jimmy yawned. "What do you mean 'first thing'? I was out at the Palladium, dancing all night. Then I went straight to the office. I haven't been home yet. Guess I should get some sleep soon, but there's a party uptown I wanna go to. Some penthouse on Riverside Drive, in the nineties. By the way, this was waiting in the telex this morning."

He reached inside his jacket and handed Jessup a rolled-up sheaf of yellow papers. "Do I get overtime for this?"

Jessup took the papers and quickly shuffled through them. His eyes lit up as he absorbed the information.

"Let me tell you, it ain't easy squeezing information out of the Pentagon on a Friday afternoon. They close that place up tighter than a drum," Ducett went on.

"Jimmy, you're beautiful. You're a good kid." Jessup's voice was filled with glee. He went back to the first page and started reading again.

"I ain't a kid," Ducett protested, but Jessup appeared not to hear.

"I'm a big boy now," Ducett said with sarcasm.

Jessup flipped to the next page, seemingly unaware of his assistant's presence.

"Wanna see my license?"

Still no reaction.

Ducett slugged the Fixer on the shoulder. "I gotta go."

Jessup looked up. "Uh, oh, yeah. Overtime. Sure. No problem. This is exactly what I needed."

Ducett smiled deliberately. "See ya later, fats." He winked.

"You're the only person in the world who can get away with calling me that," Jessup told him.

Jimmy Ducett slugged him on the shoulder again and left the car.

Walker Jessup read through the Pentagon information several times. He still didn't know exactly what was bugging Nile Barrabas, but now at least he had a few clues. There's going to be a confrontation, he thought. It wasn't something he looked forward to.

Movement on the pier caught his eye. Two men appeared on the deck of the tugboat. He reached into the back seat for the binoculars and brought them into focus. One lit up a cigarette, listening attentively as the other spoke. The second man seemed upset, anxious. Finally he stormed back inside the cabin. The first man walked to the stern of the tug and stared over the river, puffing on his fag.

Jessup put the binoculars down, a strange chill rushing down his spine. As far as he was concerned, the papers Ducett had brought him proved that the mercenary leader's attitude toward the retired General Guetz was wrong and inexcusable. But in regard to the tugboat, Barrabas was right on. Jessup had recognized both men. He'd seen them in New Jersey. On the wrong side of the firing line.

THE WHITE VAN ARRIVED half an hour later, to Jessup's great relief. Barrabas climbed out the passenger door and slipped into the BMW.

"What's up, Jessup?"

"Are the boys all here?"

"All except Billy Two."

"I'll check at the office to see if there's any word." The Fixer gestured toward the tugboat. "I think you're right about the tug. I recognized two of them from New Jersey."

"What do you mean 'you think,' Walker? I knew it the moment I laid eyes on that boat." Barrabas tapped his fist against his stomach. "Gut instinct."

"Yeah," Jessup retorted skeptically. "Just another excuse for flying by the seat of your pants." He hesitated. "Nile, I think you should tell me about your vendetta with General Guetz."

Barrabas eyed the Texan suspiciously. "What do you mean?"

"I mean this." The Fixer reached inside his suit coat and pulled out the telex. "You got a chip on your shoulder the size of a sycamore tree just because he's the one that railroaded you into a desk job at the Pentagon after Vietnam. It's all here, Nile. You begged anyone who would listen for an overseas posting, a job as a military advisor in Africa, South America, anywhere that might give you a chance at action. And when you didn't get it, you sulked. Like a petulant kid, you didn't even show up to collect that Medal of Honor they awarded you for what you did at Kap Long. You snubbed the goddamn President of the United States, and blamed it on Guetz. Then you quit." He threw the telex into the mercenary's lap.

Barrabas's blood ran cold. He knew that if he didn't control himself he'd kill Jessup right there on the spot. He picked up the papers and crushed them in his fist. His ears were ringing, and he breathed heavily. He ground his teeth together, then fumbled for the door handle, speechless and incapable of answering Jessup's accusation.

Savagely he pushed the door open and stepped out.

"Jessup." The white-haired warrior leaned into the car, brandishing the sheaf of paper. He threw it in the Fixer's face. "Do us both a favor. Stick it up your ass."

He slammed the door and stalked off.

Jessup lowered his head against the steering wheel in utter exhaustion, his face buried in his hands.

ON AN ELEGANT STREET in the Upper East Side, Deke Howard looked at the address scrawled on the crumpled slip of paper and compared it to the number on the door of the gray stone town house before him. Self-consciously, he rubbed his chin, feeling the two days' growth of whiskers, and looked down at his stained trousers, worn jacket and scuffed boots. He wasn't used to being in that kind of neighborhood. Summoning up his courage, he trotted up the steps and rang the bell.

A butler appeared and stared at him wordlessly with a disdainful expression.

"D-Deke Howard," the veteran stammered. "General Guetz asked me to—"

"Ah, yes. Mr. Howard." The butler opened the door wider and stood back. "He's expecting you."

There was something about the extravagance of luxury that created silence, Howard thought as the servant led him through the town house. It was the sensation of his feet sinking into the thick pile carpet, the fresh flowers everywhere, the rich polished wood paneling and the light glistening across the surfaces of oil paintings. It made him nervous.

The butler stopped beside oak double doors and turned to him. "Wait here a moment, if you will."

He slid back the doors and entered. Deke heard him say, "Mr. Howard, sir." The general's answer was inaudible, and a moment later the butler reappeared. "General Guetz will see you now. This way, please."

The butler led him into an oak-paneled drawing room with a low-beamed ceiling. Heraldic crests had been painted over a white marble fireplace, and the walls were hung with military portraits of long-dead heroes. Guetz walked across the room with his hand outstretched and an effusive smile on his face. He wore a maroon silk smoking jacket and gray pants.

"Deke, come in. Sit down." He motioned toward an overstuffed sofa. "Drink?"

"Uh—" Deke looked at the sofa and brushed the seat of his pants before sitting. "No, thanks, sir."

The general sat back in a wing chair across from him, crossed his legs and folded his hands on one knee. "Well, let's get right to the point, Deke. I know you're wondering why I asked you here. Would you mind telling me what happened on the New Jersey waterfront the other day?"

Howard flinched. It was the one thing that he had hoped and prayed would not be brought up. How in hell had the general found out? he asked himself and the fates that had cursed his life. He twisted his hands together nervously, keeping his eyes on them. His throat was dry.

"I, uh...I guess I made a mistake," he said weakly. Suddenly his words came in a torrent, stumbling in his hasty effort to apologize. "I didn't mean...I—I'm sorry if the Liberty Tribune is involved because of me...." He stopped to catch his breath.

"Calm down, Deke," Guetz told him. It was an order. The general stood and walked to a table against the wall where glasses stood beside crystal decanters. He poured himself a drink of amber liquid and added seltzer.

"Scotch," he explained, waving the glass at Deke. "Sure you won't have one?"

Howard nodded. The general poured a second glass.

"The so-called Argentineans who approached you were in fact Iranians. You were suckered, Deke. Taken in. You helped them steal explosives from those warehouses, and Lord only knows what act of terrorism they have planned now. Or how many innocent people will die. I have my people working on it night and day. So far, the Liberty Tribune has come out of all this intact. But it could get worse. Much worse. However, I'm going to give you a chance to redeem yourself, Deke."

"Y-you are?" Deke said with surprise, taking the glass of Scotch the general proffered. Guetz sat back in the wing chair again.

"You realize who's behind the Iranian scam, don't you?"

Howard sipped the Scotch and felt with relief the fiery liquid ease its way down his throat. He shook his head, puzzled.

"This man Nile Barrabas. You know him?"

"Not Barrabas." Deke shook his head emphatically. "He was—I knew him in Nam." He almost giggled, the idea seemed so silly. "There's no way he—"

"Deke!" Guetz snapped at the veteran. "I have conclusive information. Incontrovertible. From the highest sources. Barrabas is an embittered man. Lord knows why: we all went through the same experiences. War changes people. It changed you." Guetz's voice softened. He spoke slowly. "Didn't it, Deke?"

Howard nodded slowly. He looked down at his drink, unable to meet the general's piercing gray eyes.

"What do you want me to do?"

The retired general opened the drawer of a small round table next to the wing chair and took out a Walther P-38. He set it on the coffee table in front of Deke, giving him a careful look. Slowly he reached into the drawer again and took out an eight-round magazine. He laid it on the table beside the pistol.

"I want you to kill him."

"I—I can't," Howard stammered in protest. He stood, recoiling from the gun on the table in front of him.

"Deke! Sit down!" the general commanded.

The veteran hesitated, looking around in confusion.

"Sit, Deke!"

Slowly, he sat.

The general leaned forward, resting his forearms on his knees and cradling his drink between his hands. He spoke in gentle, persuasive tones.

"This thing could rip the Liberty Tribune wide open, Deke, if your involvement in what happened in

New Jersey becomes known. Everything we've worked for. Everything we believe in. Gone. All because of you. Already fifteen innocent men are dead. And it's Barrabas who's responsible. Think, Deke. Think. How many more will die? How can you stand to have more blood on your hands?''

Howard shuddered as if someone had plunged a knife into his gut.

"You must do it!" the general whispered. "For freedom. For democracy. For everything we believe in. There's no one else I can rely on."

Deke Howard looked at the gun. "You have proof that it's Barrabas?"

"A madman who will do anything to destroy America. Yes, Deke. I have proof." Guetz paused for only a moment. "Take the gun," he urged.

Abruptly, almost angrily, the veteran reached forward and picked up the P-38 and the magazine, rising to his feet at the same time. He stuffed the pistol in his jacket.

"Very good," Guetz said, standing. He reached into the pocket of his smoking jacket and handed Deke a small piece of paper. "Tomorrow morning. Eight o'clock. Here's an address. Ask him to meet you on the roof of this abandoned building. It will be safe for you there, I've had it checked out. No one will see. It'll be just another body, dead of a bullet wound, no motive known. Just like several others every day in New York."

Howard took the address, looking away, still unable to meet the general's piercing eyes.

"I'll have James show you out," Guetz said, pushing a button on the side table. Instantly the butler appeared at the door. The general extended his hand. Howard shook it quickly and left the room.

The retired general slowly sank back in his wing chair, watching the veteran go. He swilled the scotch in his glass and sipped.

Dale Switzer suddenly appeared at the door of the drawing room. Guetz motioned for him to enter. The man with the scarred face approached with a cocky, self-confident gait.

"Make sure that everything goes as planned in your area of responsibility," the general began. "My meeting tomorrow is very important."

"It won't be a problem," Switzer said casually. He pulled a pair of kid gloves from his jacket pocket. "These reinforcements Barrabas has brought in—that team of mercenaries—they won't try nothing. Not when they see what we've got to stop them." He motioned with a jerk of his head toward the door to indicate the departed Deke Howard. "Which one do you think will survive their little rendezvous?"

"Howard has the advantage of surprise." The general's voice was calm and even. "But this Nile Barrabas is an old war-horse. He's formidable. Like me."

"Don't matter," Switzer laughed, pulling on the gloves. "Either way, the survivor gonna have a serious accident. Like me."

DALE SWITZER PARKED HIS CAR in front of a burned-out tenement on Third Street. Graffiti had been scrawled across the crumbling facade. The last vestiges of daylight were fading quickly from the deepening dusk. Rats scuffled in the garbage and rubble of an abandoned lot. In a few windows farther down the street, lights glowed dimly through tightly closed curtains. The street was deserted.

Flashlight in hand, he made his way quickly to Avenue C and turned left, his eye on an abandoned, five-story building. The windows had been filled in with cinder blocks, and sheets of metal were nailed over the wood doors. A heavy padlock held together two ends of a heavy iron chain. Quickly he slipped a key from his pocket and opened the improvised lock. He pushed into the black interior. The acrid smell of charred wood mingled with the musky odor of ancient plaster. There was a sound of tiny scurrying feet over the cracked floors. He flicked on the flashlight. The sharp round beam threw ghostly shadows into the far corners of the ruined interior.

The floor was littered with rags and broken plastic syringes. For years, the empty tenement had been used by rubbies and winos and junkies who turned the empty hallways and apartments into shooting galleries—places where they could inject heroin, the soiled needles passing from arm to arm. Then Dale Switzer had repossessed the building for its wealthy owner—an important contributor to the Liberty Tribune's treasury. Twice he drove the junkies out. Twice they returned. Third time lucky. He smiled at the memory. He came in with some of his buddies, kicked ass, broke a few bones. Deep in their heroin stupor, the drug addicts were easy prey. He had grabbed one at random, a pale white boy who was stricken with terror.

They had taken him to a nearby abandoned lot, doused his feet and hands with gasoline and stuffed a gasoline-soaked rag into his mouth. They warned him that henceforth the same fate would be meted out to anyone discovered inside the empty building. Then they lit him. The junkies never returned.

Switzer smirked at the memory and moved stealthily up the rotting stairs to the second floor. He had enjoyed giving the scum a taste of what they deserved. The discovery that torture gave him pleasure wasn't new, however. As a child, he found a perverse satisfaction in impaling flies with pins, leaving garter snakes on railroad tracks, nailing mice to tree stumps. But Vietnam was paradise. A guy could do pretty much what he wanted there.

Switzer stopped at the landing on the second floor. His closest contact with the Vietcong had been when they were on the other end of his bayonet, squirming like worms around the steel blade that pierced their guts. But one day, on a jungle patrol, he had encountered the whip. His hands rose in an involuntary gesture, and he ran his fingertips along the raised welts of scar tissue that streaked the side of his face.

The whip was a long piece of green bamboo, supported on stakes and twisted backward into a tightly coiled arc. Three or four barbed arrows were fixed to one end. The moment his foot hit the trip wire, he knew with fatal certainty.

The bamboo pole snapped forward, hurling the arrows at his chest. He ducked, saving his life. One arrow sliced open his cheek. A second one lodged in his jaw. The third one opened up his forehead. The fourth one pierced his neck, barely missing the jugular vein and trachea.

His hatred for the little Asian soldiers magnified a hundredfold, and when his wounds had healed, he demanded a return to active duty. No longer did Vietcong die with relative speed at the end of a bayonet. He chose his place, his time, his prisoners, and learned how to make men die slowly, exquisitely.

He learned the fine art of revenge well. Whatever his contempt was for these supposedly subhuman creatures he captured in the jungles of Vietnam, he could not help but feel a certain admiration for the primitive booby traps that studded the hostile landscape. The whip was only a variation on a general theme. There were, among many others, killing machines such as angled-arrow traps, spike-board pits, tilting-lid pits, Venus flytraps, trap bridges, suspended spikes and spiked logs.

At first, he was merely a student of these inventive death devices. He collected them, eagerly forwarding the bizarre trophies to the Army Foreign Science and Technology Center in Washington. Then he wrote a manual. He became a recognized expert. Finally someone high in the echelons of power recognized his singular talent. Hieronymous Guetz. General Blood and Guts. Theirs became a perfect relationship.

Switzer stepped between the joists of a ruined wall, casting his light over the remains of a second-floor apartment. An old kitchen sink and the rusting hulk of a stove leaned together against a wall. Beside them was a window covered with plywood. Carefully he lifted the plywood down.

The window opened into a narrow well barely six feet square that led three stories upward to the roof of the building. He had toyed with this idea for a long time, certain from his continued association with General Guetz that it would someday prove useful. He pushed aside the stove and sink.

Underneath he found the four-by-four metal grate of welded iron rods. He raised it from the floor, grunting with the effort. He smiled. Spikes protruded from the joints at one-foot intervals where the rods crossed. Each spike was a foot long. Enough to go through a human body. He touched his fingertip to one. It had been filed to a needle-sharp point.

He preferred this method for his chance at his victim. The first attempt, the bomb at the Majestic Hotel so many years ago, had missed its intended mark.

Slowly he dragged the spiked grate toward the open window, breathing heavily from exertion and mounting excitement.

10

Night had fallen, and the glowing lights of the city rolled and heaved on the smooth surface of the East River. For an hour, a fine, steady drizzle had fallen, and when it stopped, the black streets were slick and shiny with the reflections of red taillights.

"Colonel, what makes you think they're going to move soon?" O'Toole asked, staring at the tugboat from the window in the rear door of the white van. They had been parked half a mile away under the elevated highway all day. "Or even that they still have explosives on board?"

"They're riding low in the water. They must have a load on board. And they aren't going to sit on those explosives leisurely for a month of Sundays. Would you?" Barrabas took the binoculars away from his eyes and looked at the Irishman.

O'Toole shook his head. "No, Colonel. I'd get them planted or whatever else they're going to do with them, and get out."

"When, Liam?"

"Tonight. 'Cept there are too many cops driving around. Tomorrow? This part of Manhattan is almost deserted on Sundays, so they could move them without much risk. But we don't know what their intention is. Could be they want to load up a truck and drive it into the middle of Soho tomorrow afternoon when the streets are packed with shoppers. Too many variables.''

"Right now, it's all variables,'' Barrabas concluded. "Except for one. That's them. And they don't move without us knowing.''

Alex Nanos and Lee Hatton were sitting in the front seats of the van, their heads back and eyes closed as they tried to grab a few moments of shut-eye. This was war, Barrabas reflected, the part that every soldier knew, but no one ever saw in the movies. Long hours of boredom interspersed with moments of sheer terror. It wasn't glamorous, but it was part of the job.

"Crick in my neck," O'Toole said, flexing his arms and shoulders and twisting his head from side to side. "Shoot-outs are hell, but at least a fellow can move around a wee bit."

"I'm going to check in with Claude." Barrabas gave him a sympathetic slap on the back. "Five hundred dollars we move within twelve hours."

The red-haired Irish-American's eyes lit up. "Colonel, you're on." He grinned. "And if I'm lucky, you'll win, if you catch my drift."

A long pier had been converted to a parking lot just north of the heliport. The speed launch was moored at the end of it. The cold, dark waters of the East River roiled against the sleek fiberglass hull. The tugboat's distinctive stack was barely visible over the pier where it had docked, five hundred yards upriver to the north.

Hayes sat in the covered bridge, bundled in a heavy overcoat against the damp November chill. "Welcome aboard, Colonel. It's a little lonely out here on the river. 'Cept for a couple of friendly wharf rats as big as cocker spaniels."

Barrabas handed him a Styrofoam cup containing hot, steamy coffee. He pried the lid off a second one for himself. Hayes raised his coffee in a toast.

"To hot weather, Colonel. Born in Detroit, but I've never got used to the cold."

"This surveillance is weighing us all down. I thought I'd spell you for a while. Go below, stretch out and rest a bit."

"That's the best offer I've heard all day." Hayes patted the radio unit in the panel of the bridge. "Beck calls in over the scrambler every half hour. So far, nothing. But with the amount of explosives it takes to weight that tug down in the water, I'd say it won't be long before they make a move. They've got too much to play with to be sitting around."

"Those are my instincts, too. If they don't move by tomorrow night, though, I want you to go in the water."

The black mercenary grimaced. "Sneak up on them from underneath, have a little look-see. I tell you, Colonel. Those waters are frigidly cold. And polluted? Walking on water ain't no miracle no more, not when it comes to the East River. By the way, did you hear the weather forecast?"

Barrabas nodded. "Scattered drizzle."

"And a bank of fog rolling in off the Atlantic tomorrow morning."

"That's when I think they'll move. The longer they wait, the more likely it is that federal agents and the police are going to get in our way. They're combing the city for the perpetrators of the New Jersey explosion, especially since Jessup told them what we saw. Eventually they'll notice this tugboat sitting here, too. I'd like to get this over and get out of here before we're stumbling over each other."

Hayes rose from his seat. "That sentiment is music to my ears," he murmured with undisguised fatigue, ambling toward the stairs to the cabin.

THE DRIZZLE CONTINUED steadily most of the night, chilling the mercs in their positions. The steady monotony of falling rain was depressing. With the first light of dawn in the skies over Long Island, it stopped. Soon after, the air turned opaque with the edge of the fog bank rolling in from the North Atlantic.

Too wired on expectation to sleep more than a few minutes, Barrabas divided his time between the van, the speedboat and the chopper, where Geoff Bishop awaited his orders. It was there, at 7:00 a.m., that the radio crackled and Nate's wavering voice came through on the scrambler.

"Colonel, they're moving! This is just in from O'Toole. A two-ton truck has pulled up on the pier. They're transferring crates into it from the tug."

"We're on alert, Nate. Tell Claude and stay tuned." Barrabas turned to Bishop. "Warm it up!"

He left the heliport on foot, jogging the quarter-mile to the waiting van. Hatton and O'Toole were making last-minute weapons inspections and practicing the grip on the converted Brownings. Nanos watched the pier through the binoculars.

"How many?" Barrabas demanded. He could feel the tension and excitement welling up inside him, almost in gratitude that their inaction had ended.

"Six and a driver."

"Colonel," Lee Hatton called from the front seat. She held out the radio earphones. "Nate. It's urgent."

Barrabas took them.

"Colonel, just had a message from Jessup. This guy, Deke Howard, contacted him. He wants a meeting with you. Apparently it's an emergency. The guy sounded desperate."

"Where?"

Nate gave him an address on Avenue C. Alphabet City. "On the roof. The downstairs door will be unlocked. He'll be there at eight."

Quickly Barrabas mentally ran over the possibilities. Deke Howard was not a well man. Did he want to give Barrabas information, or was it just a neurotic impulse, a need for attention?

He turned to O'Toole. "How fast are they moving?" He gestured toward the tug.

"Slow," the Irishman said. "I think they know what they're doing. Those crates are heavy, and dropping one would set off the others. Bye-bye tugboat, truck, pier, elevated highway, and it'll rain Iranians over downtown Manhattan in little bits and pieces."

"Colonel?" Nate Beck's voice buzzed in his ear again. "I just checked something. That address this guy Howard gave—it's on the list of properties I gave you.''

That clinched it. "Okay, Nate. I'll be there.''

"Alone, Colonel?''

"They're moving explosives from the tug, Nate. I want everyone else in position. Over and out.'' He handed the earphones back to Hatton.

"Something's come up,'' he told the other mercs. "I'll be back in short order.''

"What if they move?'' O'Toole asked.

"You know what to do. Follow them. I want to know where they plan on taking that stuff. Then we eliminate them.''

IN THE EARLY MORNING HOUR, with wisps of low-lying cloud floating in the air, the streets of Manhattan were virtually deserted. Barrabas flagged a taxi, and less than ten minutes later got out at the corner of Avenue B and Sixth Street. He checked his watch. He had half an hour for his own reconnaissance before the appointed rendezvous with Deke Howard.

Occasionally people passed on the sidewalk, walking alone or in pairs, their faces pallid from all-night bouts at one of the city's nightclubs, eyes glazed from drugs, alcohol or mere fatigue. No one noticed the tall white-haired man in dark clothing who strode quickly around the block, keeping next to facades of the buildings fronting the sidewalk and peering at the roof lines.

The building on Avenue C was abandoned, the windows sealed with cinder blocks. The chain that had locked the front doors had been recently broken. He left it and went on. Farther down the street there was another apartment house, projecting an extra story above the five-story abandoned tenements that lined the rest of the street. The outside door was open, but the inner door to the hallway was securely locked.

Barrabas took his bowie knife from a leg sheath. He jammed it forcefully into the frame beside the lock, splintering the wood. After cutting away for several minutes, he forced the knife between the bolt and the frame and pushed it back. The door opened. Quietly he made his way up six flights of stairs.

The rooftops of New York were a black-tar labyrinth of flat rectangular surfaces, ringed by the distant towers of the Manhattan skyline. In the back of the solid rows of buildings fronting the street, tiny courtyards were cut by warehouses or by empty apartment buildings long since abandoned or converted to factories, their windows bricked or sealed with sheets of tin.

Block by block, the roofs formed a maze of interlocking surfaces. The top of each building was slightly steeped toward the rear, delineated by low brick walls, the inclining planes broken by chimney pots and skylights, stairway housings leading down into interiors, and roof gardens abandoned to approaching winter. Open window wells surrounded by tile barriers took shadowy light deep into the lower floors of the buildings.

Fire escapes ran up and down the backs of the apartment buildings, metal ladders leading to more roofs above or below, where giant fans vented fumes from street-level restaurants. Razor wire, frost fences and high walls of iron bars separated one roof from another, vain attempts to stop the customary traffic of burglars who frequented the aerial pathways.

Barrabas spotted Deke Howard on a nearby roof one story below, huddling from the chill wind in the shelter of a rotting stairway housing. The veteran wore blue jeans and a tattered brown leather jacket and stood with his hands plunged deep in his pockets. His lined and tired face looked deeply troubled.

Barrabas surveyed the meeting place, two rooftops away. The cracked and brittle tar was littered with broken brick and pieces of junk. On both sides, a fence of iron bars seven feet high ran from the back of the building to the eaves overlooking the street. On the far side, the iron fence was broken by tile chimney pots protruding from a six-by-six-foot square of brick, bonded by concrete and strung with rusting razor wire. On the other side of the chimneys, there was a four-foot gap of new roofing. The iron fence, strung with coils of razor wire, continued to the eaves.

It struck Barrabas as odd that the roof of the abandoned building had been repaired. It provided too easy an access to the neighboring building, which was inhabited. A certain baffling tension squirmed in his gut, almost reminding him of something that remained elusive. He brushed it away. It was time to act.

Deke Howard glanced at his watch and paced impatiently back and forth in front of the stairs that led into the bowels of the old tenement. Quietly Barrabas ran to the edge of the roof and squatted like a griffin on the broken tiles covering the low brick wall. Propelling himself forward, he dropped ten feet to the roof below, landing quietly on cat's feet. Keeping the stairway housing between himself and Deke Howard, he ran stealthily to the eaves, and stopped next to the iron fence. Howard was barely twenty feet away, his boots scraping on the worn asphalt surface.

Carefully Barrabas gripped the bars that separated the tops of the buildings. Risking a five-story drop to certain death in the courtyard below, he swung out, pulling himself around to the other side. Razor wire scraped at his windbreaker and face. His hand clenched the bars from the other side, and he pulled himself onto the roof.

Quietly he crept to the stairway housing, his right hand gripping the modified Browning HP in the pocket of his windbreaker. Deke Howard was turned away from him, staring out at the distant Manhattan skyline. Barrabas waited for a moment, his glance darting across the patchwork of tar and fences, on the lookout for movement. He kept his back to the stairway housing, peering quickly into the stairwell through the crack between the door and the frame. It was empty. He took out the Browning and tightened his left hand around the extra grip mounted on top of the pistol.

"Howard!" he snapped.

The veteran jumped visibly at the sound of the mercenary's commanding voice. He whipped around to face Barrabas, his face shattered by fear.

"C-colonel," he stammered, catching his breath. His eyes fell to the pistol in Barrabas's hand. He took his hands from the pockets of his leather jacket and opened them like a supplicant.

"Pull out the lining!" Barrabas ordered. He watched the troubled veteran with quick, darting glances, while his eyes scanned the roofs for the least sign of motion.

Howard swallowed. He started to say something but stopped. He reached into his pocket and withdrew the P-38.

"Drop it!"

Howard threw it onto the asphalt.

"I wasn't going to use it, anyway," Howard said with resignation. "I came to warn—"

It appeared over the top of a chimney two rooftops away, a small black disembodied eye that flashed brightly for a fraction of a second. Barrabas grabbed Howard by the shoulder and threw him around the side of the stairway housing. The upper half of the rotten door shattered with the impact of the powerful 303 sniper's bullet. The two men fell on top of each other, scrambling to pull their legs into the cover of the stairway housing.

"Oh, God, oh, God," Deke mumbled deliriously, shivering violently. He was slipping into shock. A thin line of blood dripped down the side of his face. There was a gash on the side of his forehead.

Barrabas stretched out one foot and kicked at the P-38, snaring it with the toe of his boot. He pulled his foot in. The sniper's rifle sounded again, and a bullet impacted where his ankle had been. Chunks of baked, brittle asphalt showered into the air. The P-38 slithered across the tar into his hands.

Deke Howard clawed at his throat, pulling away his shirt as if he were desperate for air. His chest shook spasmodically with great hyperventilating gasps.

"Was going to warn..." he stammered, his voice cracking. "The general, general..."

"Deke!" Barrabas uttered savagely, his teeth clenched, lips tight with anger. "Deke!"

"I didn't want to. I knew it wasn't you. He lied to me. He was always lying."

"Who, Deke? Who was lying?"

"He was. He wanted me to kill you. I had to warn you, but I didn't know, I—" The crazed veteran was rambling on aimlessly, his eyes swaying back and forth in their sockets.

Barrabas grabbed him by the collar of his jacket and smashed a hand flat across his face. Deke shut up and stared at the mercenary in astonishment. His chest heaved.

Barrabas shook him furiously. "Get a hold of yourself!" he commanded. The veteran's breathing began to slow. His eyes fixed on the colonel's face, the shock in them beginning to ebb.

"Just get a hold of yourself," Barrabas repeated, slower. He relaxed his hold on Deke's jacket, and the man sank back against the wall. "Now. Who wanted me dead?"

There was another crack, and a bullet tore away a corner of the housing. The two men cringed under a shower of splinters. Deke Howard jumped nervously, banging his head against the wall and cowering from the point of impact.

"Who, Deke?"

"The General. General Guetz."

With his hand, Barrabas wiped the blood away from Deke's face. The wound in his forehead was small, probably caused by a splinter of wood.

"You with me, Deke?"

The veteran nodded. His eyes still failed to blink. Barrabas shoved the Walther P-38 into his hand. Howard stared at the gun as if he had never seen one before.

"You know how to use it, Deke!" Barrabas told him. Howard looked from the pistol to Barrabas. The mercenary twisted the veteran's finger around the trigger and closed his hand around the grip. "I'll get you out of here, Deke. But you gotta help me. I can't do it alone."

Howard looked into Barrabas's eyes and nodded.

"Can you hold him down?" Barrabas pointed to the corner of the housing. "You can cover me?"

"Yuh," Deke said in a dull whisper. He swallowed and nodded more emphatically, straightening himself and pulling his feet up. "Yeah." His voice was stronger, and his eyes had begun to clear.

"I'll circle around and get behind him. I want you to—"

"No, don't! Don't leave! You'll leave me—" He reached out, clamping his hand around Barrabas's forearm. He began to hyperventilate again.

Barrabas gripped Howard's hand and squeezed, loosening the grip. "I took care of you in Nam, Deke! Didn't I? Didn't I take care of you in Nam?"

Reluctantly Howard nodded.

"I'll take care of you here, too. But you have to trust me. Okay?"

The frightened veteran didn't react.

Barrabas leaned in close to his face and lifted Deke's hand off his arm. "Are you going to trust me, Deke?"

"Yeah," he whispered finally. Then, with more conviction, he nodded. "Yeah."

The mercenary helped Howard to his feet. They stood with their backs to the stairway housing. Deke moved slowly to the corner, the pistol up.

"I'll get us out of here," Barrabas said, his eyes on a metal ladder at the back of the roof. It led down to a fire escape. "I promise."

WITHIN MINUTES, the LongRanger helicopter rose from the heliport, with Geoff Bishop at the controls. Manhattan's skies were usually filled with a constant traffic of choppers, ferrying people from the airports to downtown, surveying road conditions for radio stations, acting as ambulances to bring in emergency patients; and there were police and Coast Guard flights. That early on a Sunday morning, however, he was alone in the sky.

He took the chopper high over the East River and went north, skirting the Brooklyn waterfront. It gave him a clear view of the tugboat on the Manhattan side without attracting attention from people on the ground. The mercs traded observations through scrambled four-way-radio conversations, and tension rose steadily. Bishop flew in a circle, crossing over Manhattan on the other side of the Brooklyn Bridge and coasting down the Hudson River. He turned at the tip of the island and had barely started up the East River again when O'Toole's voice came through the scrambler.

"They're moving."

"I read you," Bishop responded.

"Heading toward the Battery on South Street."

Bishop slowed the acceleration and hovered high over the East River. The fog banks moving in from the Atlantic pushed ominously against the Long Island shore, but didn't yet threaten Manhattan. The Iranians' two-ton truck emerged from under the elevated highway, turning west and disappearing behind a wall of skyscrapers.

"I have them," Bishop spoke slowly into the radio. "Going west on Whitehall Street."

"Got it," O'Toole answered. The van proceeded down South Street, waiting for further directions from the chopper.

Bishop increased altitude and moved over Manhattan, lining up his line of sight with the canyon of office buildings below. The truck was the only thing moving in the financial district. It turned right and headed north on Broadway. Once again, Bishop increased velocity and turned the chopper until he was looking straight up the wide avenue that split Manhattan in two.

The truck plodded slowly north under the steady stone gaze of the towering office buildings. Two blocks up, it veered left. Bishop noted the tall blackened spire of an old stone cathedral thrusting up from the office buildings that surrounded it. He radioed the landmark to O'Toole, once again throttling up and turning the chopper.

After a short pause, O'Toole's voice wavered through the scrambler, edged with excitement. "Wall Street!"

Bishop whistled. The LongRanger was positioned facing east, and he looked down into the narrow canyon in the heart of the financial district. Formerly the site of the fortress wall that surrounded the original settlement of New Amsterdam, Wall Street was unlike any other street in New York. It curved and wound between twenty- and thirty-story buildings in perpetual shadow, barely wide enough for two cars to pass each other. From the high altitude of the chopper, the tiny truck appeared to move at a snail's pace. It disappeared around a bend in the street.

Bishop twisted the throttle with his left hand and adjusted the collective. The chopper shot forward, gaining speed over Manhattan. Suddenly he was looking straight down on the narrow street. The truck made the first right turn and pulled over to the left. It stopped. The street it was on was even narrower than Wall Street. By angling to one side, he noted that the blank walls of the buildings facing it were broken by wide loading bays at street level. It was a service lane.

The airman radioed directions to the van, moving left to examine the stone skyscraper where the Iranians had parked. Far below, he could make out a classical facade of high Corinthian pillars. Whatever it was, it looked important. The white van was barely a speck against the dark gray pavement. It turned right and labored onto Wall Street.

"Got it, Geoff," O'Toole's voice snapped through the earphones in a field of static.

The Iranians had left the truck and gathered on the sidewalk in preparation for unloading, tiny little men the size of ants. "It's bad isn't it?" Bishop said, tension creeping up from his gut.

O'Toole's voice was grim, even through the scrambler's distortion. "Financial nerve center of the free world. The New York Stock Exchange."

11

Keeping the stairwell housing between him and the sniper, Barrabas crouch-walked to the edge of the roof and silently climbed down the ladder to the fire escape one story below. There was another gunshot from the roof above, followed by the voice of the would-be assassin.

"There's no escape, Barrabas. We got you. We got you any way you look at it."

Deke answered with a shot from the P-38. It pinged against the chimney, smashing brick into a cloud of fragments and ricocheting harmlessly away.

"Deke!" the assassin shouted. "Just step away from him. We don't want you. We want him."

There was a warehouse behind the abandoned tenement, running almost the length of the block. Farther down, an adjoining roof led to a fire escape and from there to the roof of the building behind the sniper. The only thing between Barrabas and his quarry was the six- or seven-foot gap to the warehouse roof.

"Hey, Deke!" the assassin shouted. "Deke! Bring him in for us. We're not gonna hurt you. C'mon. Turn Barrabas over."

The answer was another blast from the P-38.

Good boy, Deke, Barrabas silently congratulated him. He climbed onto the metal rail and jumped. As soon as his feet left the fire escape, he realized that he wasn't going to make it. He reached desperately, grabbing for the top of the low wall that surrounded the warehouse roof. His hands gripped the tile, curling around it like pincers, and his body slammed into the brick wall. He strained, scraping the skin off his face as he pulled himself slowly up, inching his torso higher until finally he was hanging half on top of the low wall. With an immense effort, he swung his legs up and over, and rolled onto the tar surface.

On the roof of the abandoned building, the sniper fired again. The bullet hit and pinged off into space.

"I'm not waiting any longer!" Switzer bellowed, his anger rising. "You got thirty seconds. Then I'm coming after you!"

Deke listened behind the cover of the stairwell housing, his breathing nervous and irregular, his head swimming in sweat. The field of tar and crumbling brick wavered and circled in front of his eyes. He shook his head, trying to clear his vision, but the roof was gone now, and in its place there was a green jungle, thick with verdure, tropical plants shivering with terror, long wispy vines hanging like temptation from the canopy of leaves.

He knew where he was—crouched behind a rotting tree with the patrol pinned down by the Vietcong ambush on the Kap Long River. Colonel Barrabas had run along the shore and crossed the stream upriver, to circle in behind, and Deke had volunteered to go downriver, riding the edge of a razor-sharp knife.

And there they were, hunched behind an embankment of rotting vegetation, as were the little men in black pajamas, both groups firing at one another across the river. And there was Deke, M-16 in one hand, Colt in the other, a one-man army with bullets to spare. He remembered his instructions: when you hear the colonel, start shooting....

The flashback blinked out as suddenly as its onset. Howard shook his head, not believing any more what his eyes saw. It was November, a chill, dull morning on a rooftop in New York City, and a man was firing a gun at him again. *Shoot when you hear the colonel.*

"Hey, Barrabas, Deke!" the assassin taunted. "I'm coming! I'm coming for you!"

The rifle snorted twice, and bullets pounded into the corner of the stairway housing, blowing away chunks of wood. Switzer jumped from his hiding place and zigzagged across the roof, the foam soles of his boots silent on the asphalt. He raised the rifle and fired again at the housing, then jumped behind the chimney of the abandoned building.

He flattened himself against the brick. "C'mon, Barrabas. Come and get me!"

Deke Howard held his breath, his ears straining to hear the footsteps of the assassin. Switzer was closer, and more to the left, a silent creeping enemy, hiding behind the massive brick bulwark that contained the chimneys. Where in hell was the colonel?

"Shoot-out time," Switzer leered. "C'mon over and take me out!"

Howard rose to his feet and held the P-38 across his chest. He crept close to the corner of the housing.

What the hell, he thought. I can't let another good man die.

One building away, the mercenary sprang to his feet and loped along the graveled roof, then jumped down several feet to the roof on the second building, scrambling over giant pipes and dodging the huge exhaust installation from a ground-floor restaurant. Urban warfare. It was an obstacle course. The city was a jungle of geometries, a complex of nests and lairs constructed of cold steel, smooth glass, hard stone, twisted metal, made by man challenging nature, to be challenged by him. But war was the same all over....

He'd taken two men with him into the fetid steaming jungle of Vietnam, crawling on their bellies through slime and impenetrable rain forest, slipping through ever-tighter perimeter lines into a hellish land. Weighted boards bristling with barbed spikes dropped from the obscurity of overhead greenery, nailing six inches through the skull of one of Barrabas's men. A steel arrow, its catch mechanism released by a tugged trip wire, fired through bamboo that was angled in a little pit so that it drove up between the other man's legs and lodged in his heart.

Barrabas was the only one left, alone in a landscape littered with death traps. Crawling along until the ground suddenly opened beneath him, he rolled violently to one side, saving himself from the dark pit that threatened to swallow him whole. He'd glimpsed his own fate in the blackened, maggot-ridden corpse stuck with spikes below, gripped his fear in his fists and squeezed it, forcing himself to go on. General

Chan Minh Chung's command center had been less than a mile away....

He leapt onto the fire escape, climbed one flight, taking two rungs at a time, barely touching each step with the toes of his boots. He jumped at the rungs of the ladder that led to the roof, his arms pulling him higher while his legs kicked at the rungs below.

When his head was level with the edge, he took the Browning from his pocket. Scrambling up the last rung, he burst over the top, the pistol out in front. His left hand grabbed the second handle as his leg went forward. He searched for the target, his finger leaning on the trigger.

Switzer stood in the open behind the chimney. He swung around, bullets belching from the fiery muzzle of his rifle. Suddenly Deke Howard appeared from nowhere, holding his pistol in a two-handed grip. He jumped to the top of the chimney, blasting as he went.

Switzer yelped. Blood appeared along his arm from elbow to wrist. The rifle jumped from his hands and smashed to the roof, skittering across the asphalt and coming to a stop at Barrabas's feet.

The merc bent down and took the weapon, keeping the Browning trained on Guetz's hired assassin. His eyes met Deke's in silent, understood thanks. Deke, white-faced with fear, gave a slight nod. He jumped down to the roof, covering Switzer from the other side with his P-38. The assassin stepped sideways, clenching his wounded forearm with the other hand. Blood seeped through his fingers and dripped on the tar. He looked in confusion from Barrabas to the rifle, edging away.

"Back off!" Switzer bawled desperately, shielding himself with his crossed arms. He was breathing hard to fend off the pain, but his eyes cleared, and suddenly he was trying to laugh at them.

"Just back right off, boys," he sneered, edging closer to the door to the stairs. "'Cause we got your girlfriend, Barrabas. Anything happens to me—she's history, man. She's dead!"

IN THE WHITE VAN, Liam O'Toole and Lee Hatton pored over a map of the financial district. Nanos drove, following the Iranians' truck up Broadway just as it turned into Wall Street.

"We can't just start shooting!" the Greek cried. "Not when they're sitting on half a ton of unstable explosives."

"He's right," O'Toole muttered. His forehead was furrowed with concentration as he examined the maze of streets that made up the heart of the world's trading center. "We have to get them running away from the truck."

"Here," Hatton said, stabbing her finger at the map. "If we keep going down Wall Street, we can circle around and come back at them from the other side."

"What good will that do?" O'Toole asked. "Unless we put someone at the top of Wall Street to drive them south."

"That's what I mean. And maybe Geoff can ride their tail. My bet is they'll run on foot rather than try for it in a slow-moving truck weighed down with volatile explosives. They were handling those cases pretty gingerly on the dock. They'd be fools to risk it. And after I get them heading south, you block the intersection at Hanover Street, forcing them north. I cut across down Wall Street to here...." She put her finger on the map.

"You mean—" A smile spread slowly across Liam O'Toole's Irish mug as Lee's ingenuity sank in.

He grabbed the microphone and called the chopper.

From the cockpit of the Bell LongRanger, Bishop examined the vertical stone walls of office buildings that formed the canyon of streets in the financial district.

"I can ride their ass a bit," he spoke into the radio to O'Toole. "But the rotor will set up a lot of turbulence against the sides of these buildings. It'll have to be short and sweet. But it'll scare the hell out of them."

"We'll take care of the rest," O'Toole promised.

"I have first dibs," Lee told her fellow mercs in a tone of voice that left little room for discussion. She shouldered her M-16 and crouched by the side door in anticipation.

Liam O'Toole was about to assert his rank as second in command but stopped. "Sure you don't want some help?"

Lee shook her head emphatically. "I can handle it. You two take care of the welcoming committee at the other end."

Nanos turned onto Wall Street, maintaining a steady speed of thirty miles an hour. In the weak gray light of early morning, a fine light drizzle had started.

The mercs drove past New Street, craning their necks to spy on the Iranians through the tinted windows.

A team of six men, wearing dark overalls, worked in two groups. They carried crates from the truck, setting them carefully on an electric dolly at the entrance to a loading dock. Nanos braked quietly in front of the stock exchange, and Lee Hatton opened the side door and stepped out, cradling the M-16 carefully. She patted the extra magazines in her jacket pocket for reassurance, closed the door quietly and ran back toward the corner of New Street. The clip-clop of the approaching helicopter grew more distinct.

Nanos eased the van away from the curb and drove faster. Wall Street curved past an immense construction sight that took up most of the next block. A half-dozen cement trucks lined the curb, churning away. Under the supervision of a few yellow-hatted construction workers, tons of concrete slush gushed down sixty-feet-long slides into the foundations. The hard hats lounged around the opening in the plywood fence, bored and earning eighty dollars an hour.

They cast suspicious glances at the white van speeding past and turning south on Pearl Street.

"There!" O'Toole pointed to a street angling sharply to the right. "Beaver Street."

The towering office buildings were gone. For a few small blocks, there were three- and four-story houses, scattered remnants of Manhattan a hundred years ago. Nanos veered sharply left and braked. The van blocked the southbound exit of the intersection at Hanover Street. Aside from the terrorists and the construction workers, they hadn't passed another human being.

The rapid chop of the helicopter's rotor reverberated between Manhattan's skyscraper canyons. Bishop lined up a clear view of the truck and the tiny stick men who unloaded its deadly cargo on New Street. He lowered the collective, automatically adjusting the throttle to maintain rpm. The LongRanger dropped like a stone.

He flew in low over the roof of a Greek temple, where a giant bronze statue of George Washington stared benignly on the stock exchange. Down the street, the Iranians looked up from their work. The chopper came in fast, the *whop-whop-whop* of its rotor blades echoing against glass and steel cliffs on both sides.

Bishop sank to forty or fifty feet, the sound of his engines almost deafening. Lee Hatton waited, pressed against the corner of the stock exchange. The chopper flashed past, swung down to the third-story level and rose like a pendulum in the airspace over New Street.

The Iranians froze, terrified by the aircraft that appeared from the November gray like a preternatural bird of prey. Hatton spun around the corner, sinking to one knee. The M-16 was on full auto. She closed on the trigger of the submachine gun, aiming high to keep the fire well away from the dangerous crates.

The terrorists ran from the crates toward the truck, scrambling over one another to pile into the cab. Several dove into the back, pulling the doors shut behind them. Two fought to get in the passenger door.

"Damn," Hatton cursed. Now the SOBs had a problem. If the van blew, there would be a hell of a mess. She sighted down the scope of the M-16 again, this time zeroing in on a moving target. Gore exploded across the chest of one man, knocking him out of the competition. The other man by the door grabbed the body and hauled it into the cab. The engine roared, and the truck pulled into the street, careering wildly from curb to curb.

"They went for the truck," Bishop warned O'Toole via the radio. "I'll turn them your way if you still want them."

The copper soared high over the roofs of the buildings again, turning in a full circle. Bishop again dropped the collective. His stomach fluttered around his throat as the chopper dipped. The wind stream smacked against the sides of the office towers, shaking the thick glass windows with a sound like thunder. The LongRanger vibrated from the strange turbulence, the engine sinking and recovering as errant winds battered the fuselage.

He hit his low point at the third story of the office buildings again, lifted the collective and swooped over the hood of the fleeing truck. The escaping terrorists panicked, veering left onto Exchange Place, fishtailing wildly. The driver accelerated.

O'Toole and Nanos waited behind the white van at the end of the street.

"If they ram us and the van explodes—" the Irish American began angrily.

"We're goners. Liam, look there." Nanos pointed up Hanover Street to where it met Wall Street, facing the block-long construction sight. The fence had been removed to make way for the cement chutes. "With Lee on one side and me on the other—"

"Go for it!" O'Toole snapped. "I'll send them your way, I promise!"

Nanos dashed from behind the van, his legs flying beneath him, heading up the fifty-yard stretch toward Wall Street. Liam O'Toole shouldered his automatic rifle and sighted along Exchange Place. The truck veered crazily around the corner. The two-ton death vehicle came on, its engine roaring and gears grinding. The driver shifted up.

"Holy shit," O'Toole exclaimed. The truck was on a ramming course, heading straight for the side of the white van.

"BACK OFF, BARRABAS, if you fucking wanna see your girlfriend alive again," Switzer taunted, gleefully aware of the expression on the mercenary's face.

Barrabas was burning, denying it was possible but knowing that battlefields hold no jokes.

"Name's Anna, isn't it? Anna Kulikowski. The general's boys are over there getting her right now." Switzer laughed, displaying a wide row of teeth. He continued edging toward the door to the stairs. "You hurry, you might get there in time to stop them. We both go back the way we came. You go that way."

He jerked his head toward the roof of the abandoned building next door. There was only one easy way over—across the square of new roofing. Switzer gestured the other way toward the stairs.

"I'll go the way I came in. Through here."

Barrabas planted his legs apart and aimed the Browning horizontally, gripping both handles and leaning forward against the recoil. He fired once.

The bullet nicked the toe of Switzer's boot and pounded into the tar. The assassin jumped back.

"No deal!" Barrabas shouted. "You go that way!"

He fired again, holding the trigger down. Switzer hopped across the roof, yelping with fear as the bullets exploded at his feet, scraping the tops of his boots.

"No!" he screamed, almost begged, putting his hands out to stop the deadly fire and dancing backward.

"Get the hell out!" Barrabas yelled. He went down on the trigger again.

Bullets clipped Switzer's trouser cuffs and tore a chunk from the leather at his ankle. He turned and fled, running in panic for the next roof. Suddenly a patch of roof disappeared beneath his feet. His horrible screams wound like livid snakes from the neat square hole.

Barrabas walked to the edge, with Deke Howard following reluctantly.

The window well led deep into the bowels of the abandoned building. At the bottom, Switzer lay pinned like an insect on top of the thin roofing, iron stakes through his arms, legs, body, neck, his head gleaming with blood. Dale Switzer, wide-eyed and dead, the perpetrator of his own impalement.

The body would rot, food for rats and cockroaches, frozen in winter, the summer stink indiscernible among the normal stench of New York garbage and debris. Deke Howard dropped to his knees, weeping and shaking violently, his face buried in his hands.

"I hate this, I hate it all," he gasped, his chest heaving as he fought for air between deep body-wrenching sobs. "I even hate crying. I'd rather be a statue. Statues never have to feel anything."

"It's okay, Deke." Barrabas rested his hand on Howard's back. "This is what he intended for us. It's over now. Vietnam is really over."

All of a sudden the mercenary noticed that a fine cold drizzle had begun, with slivered raindrops as sharp as tiny needles.

12

Nate Beck sat at a console of monitors in the center of the vast office space, the windows on three sides staring at Manhattan from the fiftieth floor. Listening through the radio to the conversation in the van, he watched the helicopter swoop down and disappear into a canyon of buildings several blocks away. A light on the board in front of him blinked. He flicked a toggle switch. The infrared audio-sensor beam had picked up something interesting.

The voice sounded tinny, but it was clearly the voice of the general Nate had heard on news tapes. Guetz. In the World Trade Center offices of the Liberty Tribune, he was entering his office, speaking with another man.

"The rest of the board members will be here in less than an hour. Tell me when they've arrived in the boardroom. I have some paperwork to do before the meeting." There was a muffled thud, the closing of a door.

The conversation ended.

O'TOOLE TOOK AIM with the Armalite and splattered a row of holes across the side of the truck. Part of the windshield shattered. The truck careered left, its tires screeching against the pavement in protest. The Irishman ran into the street and bore down with the rifle, taking sight at the back doors. "Let it go," he muttered to himself, lowering the weapon and remembering the explosives.

Alex Nanos was almost at the top of the street when suddenly the truck was behind him. The passenger door opened, and a man leaned out, firing. The bullets pinged into the road at Nanos's feet.

At the other end of the street, O'Toole shifted his aim from the back door to the back of the gunner and blew three rounds through him. Flattening briefly against the flapping door, the gunner teetered into the street. The driver steered wide to take the corner onto Wall Street, flipping the body under the rear wheels.

Lee Hatton ran past the startled gaze of the construction workers, who looked up from steaming cups of coffee, scarcely believing their eyes. Simultaneously Nanos broke into the open, the sound of his footsteps exploding behind him.

Lee went down on one knee. The cab of the two-ton truck stormed to the end of Hanover Street, roaring like an enraged beast. She squeezed the trigger, with the M-16 on full auto. Bullets pounded into the driver's door. The window was obliterated. With the butt of the auto rifle pressed against his thigh, Nanos took up the refrain from the other corner, putting a seam of lead into the engine housing.

The truck lurched left and right, wildly out of control, but its forward momentum took over. It barreled blindly across the intersection. Terrified, the construction workers ran for cover behind the cement trucks. The explosive-laden vehicle plunged through the opening in the fence. For a moment, at the apex of its airborne flight, it became graceful. Then it dropped like a stone.

Hatton and Nanos froze on opposite sides of the street, waiting for the explosion.

It didn't come. They ran across the street to the edge of the construction site. The pit was indeed deep. Half of it was covered with a giant maze of crisscrossed steel. The other half was a vast pool of semiliquid concrete. The truck was sinking into it, farting air bubbles when the top of the cab slipped beneath the souplike surface. A plume of watery cement fell from a chute and sprayed the roof of the cab.

"D-don't shoot," a frightened voice chattered near them. The construction workers, six of them, cowered behind the nearby cement truck, their hands open in supplication.

"We don't see nothing—you tell Mr. Genovese," their leader assured them anxiously. "Mr. Genovese very great man. He bless my granddaughter. We see nothing." He shook his head and shrugged like an innocent. "Nothing."

"'Mr. Genovese'?" Lee said to Alex.

"Yeah, a local mob family of good standing."

"Nothing!" The hard hat threw his arms into the air with a hearty smile, looking from one merc to the other. "Sunday morning. Nothing else."

The white van screeched to a halt in front of them, and O'Toole waved frantically from behind the wheel. In the distance was the wail of police sirens.

"Let's get out of here, Lee." Alex began edging toward the van.

Hatton looked at the construction workers and brandished the rifle. "Genovese!" she affirmed in the deepest voice she could muster. The hard hats nodded eagerly, shaking their fingers appreciatively at the female warrior. She followed Alex and hopped into the back of the van.

BARRABAS RAN, gasping air into lungs already raw from exhaustion. His legs flew beneath him across Thompkins Square Park. In a single bound he leapt across the bodies of skinheads lounging on the sidewalk of Avenue A. In a semiconscious state somewhere between "up" and "down," this planet and another one, they scarcely noticed, and nodded back to where they came from.

He swung around the corner onto First Avenue, and suddenly it was in front of him, the entrance of Anna's building. He aimed the pistol for the lock, but kicked instead. It swung listlessly inward, the lock already broken. He flew up the stairs. Her apartment door was closed. Beyond it, he heard her shrieks of panic and fear, barely muffled by the walls.

"Anna! Anna, it's me!" But he didn't wait for her to come. "Stay away from the door!" he shouted, firing twice into the lock. He burst through the door and saw her struggling with a man in the living room. A second man was climbing in the window from the roof. Anna's assailant threw her savagely against the wall, then swept around, his pistol aimed at Barrabas's face. With a smooth and continuous motion,

Barrabas brought the Browning out in front, both hands gripping tightly. Anna grabbed a table lamp and smashed it against the thug's gun, and it fired.

Hot, steely pain lanced through Barrabas's leg. Barrabas squeezed the trigger on the Browning once. A deafening blast shook the room, and a third eye, round and red, opened in the gunman's forehead.

The man at the window scrambled to get back on the roof. There was a broom leaning against a corner of the room, and Barrabas grabbed it as though it was a javelin. With a growl of fury, he ran across to the open window and shoved it into the snatcher's gut.

The man screamed a desperate protest, his foothold giving way. He hung from the eaves, his body swinging wildly back and forth.

"Who sent you?" Barrabas demanded. He punched the broomstick into the man's stomach again, pushing him away from the building.

"No!" the assailant begged, his legs thrashing for something solid to rest on. "Guetz sent us! General Guetz! To get the girl! Not to kill her!"

Barrabas slammed the wooden staff into the hoodlum again. "Where is he!"

"I dunno!" The man flexed his arms in a mad attempt to lift himself onto the roof. Barrabas plowed the end of the broomstick into his stomach again. The man's body sagged, his fingers barely holding on. The eavestrough broke away from the corner of the building, bending under the man's weight. He hung precariously in midair. He shrieked with inarticulate terror.

"Where the hell is he!" Barrabas demanded. He jabbed the broomstick into the assailant, making him swing more.

"The offices. World Trade Center!" the hoodlum shrieked, curling his body against the poking broomstick. It was the last instinctive reflex he ever had. Several more feet of trough broke from the eaves, swinging him farther away from the building. He bounced in midair, squirming like a worm at the end of a hook. His fingers gave out. He let go. His long, shrill scream plummeted with him, punctuated by the finality of a thud five stories below.

Barrabas heard nothing. Nothing sounded different from silence. It pressed against his ears, and the room, which was swimming around his head, had the still clarity of absolute perfection. His right leg was numb, and when he looked down, it was a sheet of blood. He saw Anna kneeling on the rug, her face stained by tears, her long dark hair in disarray.

He knelt beside her, taking her hand and looking into her eyes, loving her, and his arms closed around her fear-racked body. She hesitated, shivering with the residue of terror, but surrendered finally to his embrace, burying her face against his chest and sobbing.

"It's okay, baby." He kissed the side of her head and helped her to the couch, his leg feeling like a block of ice seared with a red-hot poker. When Anna sat, he said, "Everything will be taken care of."

He limped painfully to the telephone and dialed Walker Jessup's special number. The Texan answered with a yawn.

"Jessup, I made a mess. I need some of your Company specialists to clean it up. Fast. Before the police get here."

"What in hell..." The Fixer mumbled sleepily. He sat up in bed. "What happened?"

"They went for my girlfriend! Now can you get someone here?" He gave Jessup the address.

"Who— Never mind." The Fixer's voice sounded fully alert. "Give me five minutes to get there, Nile. Someone else will be over to clean up. Make sure you're not around."

The phone clicked. Barrabas went into the bedroom and ripped a sheet from the rumpled bed. He tore a wide strip and bent to tend to the wound in his leg. The bullet had pierced his thigh, tearing through a chunk of muscle not far from the bone. He bound a strip of sheet tightly around his leg where it met his groin, squeezing the main artery and stemming the flow of blood.

The pain was incredible, yet somehow he felt detached from the reality of his own maimed body. He wrapped a wide strip tightly around the wound and tied the ends. Blood blossomed through the layers of improvised bandage. The leg felt heavy, as if half his body rested on an upright log, but he could walk. He grabbed what was left of the sheet to throw over the dead man in the living room. He was aware of Anna's scent wafting up from the soft cotton.

"Too good!" he cursed, throwing it down and stumbling to the living room. Quickly he rolled the rug across the body. He went to the couch and put his arms around Anna.

"Someone's coming to stay with you, okay?"

She looked at him, the daze clearing from her eyes. Her brow furrowed with bewilderment. "You stay with me!" she demanded in a tone that was almost incredulous because she already knew his answer. "You will not leave me alone with the police!"

"I can't stay," he told her. "I can't be here when they come. But someone will be here any minute to take care of you. A very fat man. His name is Walker Jessup. Then I'll be back for you. I promise." He kissed her lips softly, then pulled away.

"Stay! Please!" she cried, grabbing his legs to bring him back. "I need you!"

He knelt beside the couch. "I have to take care of the person who did this to you."

She stopped crying. She merely watched him go.

He ran from the apartment, crashing unsteadily against the wall in the hall. The injured leg made his movements lopsided, and his head felt light. He gritted his teeth, descending the stairs by pushing the frozen limb ahead of him, fighting the pain that rose higher and higher, spreading through his groin like searing flames. Just as he got through the entrance, the BMW screeched to a halt at the curb, and Jessup flew from the car. He wore a suit coat over his pajama top. His glance fell to the bloody leg.

"Keys!" Barrabas demanded, opening his palm.

Jessup's mouth dropped open. He handed them over.

"Fifth floor," the warrior told the Fixer, lurching to the car.

The general wanted proof. Barrabas had had it for more than a decade. It was time to play the final hand. The next round was for the general.

THE LIBERTY TRIBUNE'S boardroom was paneled in a sand-colored veneer. The ceiling was artificially lowered, and the lights were cleverly concealed behind fake wood beams. The floor was beige marble. The eastern wall was glass, filled with a vista of the spiked towers of the financial district. Across the river, Brooklyn was obscured by low-lying fog. A fine drizzle wetted the windows. The shapeless clouds pressed lower, threatening to wrap the skyscraper in a shroud.

Five men sat in upholstered chairs at the polished walnut table, each with a china coffee cup at his place, but nothing more. None of them noticed the tiny red dot on the bottom right corner of the farthest window.

"Gentlemen," the retired general began from his position at the head of the table. "As is our usual custom, I have not supplied pads or writing implements. I need not remind any of you of the danger of committing to paper what is discussed in this room."

The four men indicated their agreement with bored nods and alligator eyes. Guetz looked around the table. They were all middle-aged but younger than him—their hair immaculate, nails manicured, faces tanned and healthy, the skin smooth from expensive emollients, and their dark suits tailored to fit perfectly. Between the four of them, they controlled fortunes greater than emperors'.

"If you are all ready, we'll go around the table. Each of you in turn will state briefly what matter you wish to discuss, and that will serve as our agenda for more detailed discussion." He looked at each stern, unsmiling face. "The industrialist first."

He nodded to the first man, who was small in stature and skinny, with a round head and short dark hair.

The man's thin wiry mustache twisted as he spoke. "Once the stock market is destroyed, we can expect economic collapse. After being closed for two days on the weekend, and subsequently wiped out indefinitely, there's no way the electronic network that holds together the complex financial records can be reactivated in time to prevent the economy from grinding to a halt. It will be the end of the bull market. The bubble will break. Millions of people will be instantly thrown out of work. No new wealth has been created in the past decade—only vast sums of money changing ownership. With the budget and trade deficits, American currency will teeter on the brink of worthlessness."

He smiled slowly, his dark eyes glinting at his colleagues. "I hope you gentlemen have already sold off your stock portfolios. I suggested gold and platinum, as you recall."

General Guetz turned to the short plump man with the dark complexion who sat next to the industrialist. "And now our Saudi friend can briefly elucidate on his business in the trafficking of arms."

The death merchant twisted his neck against his stiffly starched collar and spoke in perfect Oxford-accented English. "I have been pouring weapons into various liberation movements, guerrilla armies and terrorist organizations at an unprecedented rate, particularly in Mexico and Central America. When the American economy collapses, these organizations will be sorely tempted to strike against each other. My sales agents are in place, ready to coax them with promises of easy access to unlimited supplies."

General Guetz switched his gaze across the table, signaling a tall man with a smooth face and only a fringe of brown hair at the sides of his head. His shiny bald pate glistened under the overhead light.

"And now, perhaps our producer can fill us in on what's happening in the City of Angels."

The movie mogul cleared his throat, squirming restlessly in his chair. "We've performed well in the past few years, releasing a steady supply of Rambo-type war films, and seeing their market popularity surge incredibly. You've seen them—*Top Gun*, *Eagle Squad*, *Red Dawn*, *Heartbreak Ridge*, and that TV series about a Russian takeover. But we're scraping hard for subject matter, what with the subject of Vietnam being so tainted. Hollywood can only milk missing POWs, Grenada and imaginary Russian invasions for so long. What we need is something more substantial. A new war to sell."

He snickered. "The Russians have been angrier than hell—Pravda started calling it 'warnography.' I call it 'warno.' Ha-ha. In any event, we've managed to romanticize the warrior ethos. War is hell, but it's the only way to be a hero, and that's certainly an appealing message to millions of young men who are either unemployed or working in mindless factory-type jobs. We have a dozen more hard-hitting films in that genre, still in the can, and ready to go when you are,'' he ended enthusiastically.

General Guetz turned to the fourth man. "And in Washington?" he inquired.

The politician, white-haired and wrinkled, clasped his bony hands together on the polished table.

"The situation in Mexico is already unstable. Their economy has collapsed, their debt burden to our banks is so hopeless they can never pay it back and their currency is worthless. The government has remained in power for the previous fifty years through corruption and fraud at the ballot boxes, and the people know it. They're restless, and the socialists are moving in. In the Capitol, there's growing anxiety about our southern neighbor. Once the revolutionary groups start shooting—" he nodded appreciatively to the Saudi across the table "—and with massive unemployment and instability here in the States—"

"America will go back to work," the industrialist interjected. "A wartime economy will boom."

"The invasion of Mexico!" The movie mogul savored the delicious words, visions of screenplays in his head.

"And on, to Nicaragua, and the rest of Central America," the politician crowed, smiling broadly. "America will never be humiliated again."

A satisfied smile creased General Guetz's face. "And now, gentlemen. Shall we get down to details?"

THE MERCS GATHERED AROUND the chopper at the East River heliport. Geoff Bishop was helping a mechanic refuel the aircraft. The man kept looking up in the direction of sirens that wound frantically through the financial district several blocks away.

"They're going to be here eventually," O'Toole warned the others, "once someone tells them about a helicopter buzzing through the streets."

In the cockpit, Alex Nanos manned the radio, keeping in contact with Claude Hayes. The black man was waiting at the speedboat, ready to pick up the mercs when given the word.

Suddenly Nate Beck's voice twisted through the scrambler. He told the Greek about the meeting in the offices at the World Trade Center.

"If I didn't have it on tape, I wouldn't believe it, Alex."

"Just a second, Nate." Alex leaned from the cockpit and called to O'Toole and Hatton. They came to the window, and he repeated what he learned from Nate.

The mercs looked at each other anxiously, uncertain of the next step.

"Now we know why the colonel targeted the general," Lee said quietly, putting into words the question that had baffled all the mercs since their arrival in New York. "That's where this whole Iranian fiasco started. He must have known something else was up."

"That doesn't answer the sixty-million-dollar question here and now, though," O'Toole muttered darkly.

Nanos and Hatton looked at him.

"Where in hell's Barrabas?" he asked, worry written across his face.

13

Barrabas stood on the plaza of the World Trade Center, buffeted by wind-driven sheets of fine icy drizzle. Two square shining buildings thrust above him, each a hundred and ten stories that vanished finally into cold gray mist. His quarry was somewhere more than fifty floors overhead. He mated mag to Browning, forty new rounds. The long end protruded way out the end of the right grip. He was ready. He started walking.

Proof, the general had said. Bring proof—that's the American way. Barrabas was the proof. For the second time he stalked the general, this time knowing it. But like the last time, alone in the death-studded jungle, the closer the warrior got, the braver he became. He was crazed but not foolhardy. Fear was alien to him. It was a game, played against a demon who preyed on the living....

He'd filtered past guards, thin as shadows at dusk, inched on his belly through the muck of a mine field, backed under barbed wire like a snake cleaving grass. Finally, ragged and dirty, he slunk into the village of silent huts at night, following the noise of chatting officers and the footsteps of pacing guards.

Two of them he killed, his swift and terrible knife traveling the expanse of their naked necks, and then he peered into the general's home, where tea was being served around a low lacquered table. A cup was set before the dark visage of U.S. Army General Hieronymous Guetz, who smilingly passed the documents across the table into the long smooth hands of NV General Chan Minh Chung.

He had never had a chance to ask the general why....

The elevator's steel doors sighed and opened, and he stepped out onto the fifty-fourth floor. The elegantly appointed corridor was empty, save for the hushed breath of circulating air. The wide wooden doors with the big brass handles waiting at the end.

He knelt before the door on the left, wincing as pain shot through his wounded leg, and extracted his knife from the sheath. Digging the blade inside the edge of the other door, his hand strained on the leather handle. The door began to open.

He pushed it wider.

Bullets pounded past him at chest level. He pivoted on his left leg, swinging around the door and grabbing the second grip on the Browning. He lined up his target and fired twice.

Red roses bloomed on a man's white shirt, on either side of his tie. He spun around, dead in his tracks, collapsing on top of his gun with his butt in the air. Barrabas swung smoothly to his left and fired again. The second man caught the kiss on the ridge of his nose. It splattered from the center of his face. He fell, quivering violently while his brain short-circuited around 9 mm of lead, synapse by neuron.

Barrabas adjusted his aim for the dark glass eye that stared at him from high in the wall behind the big white desk. He fired. It blinked out with a shatter of glass. He pivoted, fired again and permanently shut a second glass eye. With fast, perfect timing, he circled, leaning against the recoil, aiming, firing, popping surveillance cameras around the circumference of the room. Splinters and shards of glass littered the impressive furniture.

The wide metal doors behind the reception desk slid open. Barrabas had a view of Manhattan floating beyond the window wall, her stone fingers clawing at the dark November sky. Thin and tattered wraiths of cloud fluttered past the windowed cliffs, looking in, and, horrified or indifferent, took flight in the arms of the constant wind.

They were there. Men with submachine guns. Two of them in the corners on either side of the room.

"Congratulations, Colonel Barrabas. You made it." General Guetz walked to the edge of the balcony at the top of the winding staircase and remained there with his hands on the railing. Behind him, through the glass wall of the boardroom, four men watched.

"And now, you'll die."

Barrabas stood, legs spread apart, and looked up at his prey. "First, we got something to settle."

NATE BECK LISTENED with growing shock to the sounds of gunfire transmitted by the infrared beam. His blood ran cold when he heard the colonel's name. He tabbed in Nanos at the heliport.

"Listen to this!" Quickly Nate changed plugs, putting the surveillance transmission through the scrambler.

"Where in hell is he?" Nanos demanded as Bishop opened the driver's door and climbed into the pilot's seat.

Hearing Nanos's excitement, O'Toole and Hatton ran to the window of the chopper and stood by.

"World Trade Center. Offices of the Liberty Tribune. He's gone in alone!"

"What in hell is going on!" Lee snapped angrily.

"No way we can get there in less than ten minutes—fifteen with elevators," O'Toole told the others.

Geoff Bishop leaned over Nanos to speak through the window. "Three by chopper."

"It's as far down from the roof as it is up from the ground," Nanos pointed out. He jerked his thumb over his shoulder. "And there's rappeling equipment, cables, a grappling hook—"

"Let's go!" O'Toole shouted. He and Hatton dove into the LongRanger. The rotor swept in faster and faster circles, lifting them from the heliport and back to the skyscraper canyons of Lower Manhattan.

GENERAL GUETZ raised his brows with mock indignation. "We both know what it is, Colonel Barrabas, if I'm not mistaken. I don't think there's much to be gained by discussing it," he said sadly. He signaled to the gunmen on either side of the room. They lowered their submachine guns slightly. The general stepped toward the top of the stairs.

"Why!" Barrabas snapped. "Why did you sell America out by giving Chan Minh Chung all the military data they needed to overrun us?"

"So you did see me there, after all!" Guetz beamed, half smiling in admiration. "I could never be certain. But when Chan Minh Chung's battle plans appeared on my desk through our own intelligence channels, I learned about your secret mission. Chan Minh Chung was furious, but he refused to believe it was anything other than an inside job. Twelve of his officers were executed. He was certain that if he killed them all the traitor would be among them."

The general snickered. "So they were as innocent as they protested, after all. Does it please you to have caused their deaths?"

"You're a traitor all decked out like an all-American hero," Barrabas shouted defiantly to the man at the top of the stairs. "A statesman with the blood of thousands of young American men on your hands."

Guetz's face reddened, and his eyes clouded with dark fury. "I did what any good soldier and officer would do when I recognized we were going to lose Vietnam! I planned a strategic retreat, one that would give us optimum strength to regroup, to take the offensive and eventually achieve final victory!"

He took a few steps downward, breathing deeply to regain his composure. "Vietnam challenged military thinking. It was necessary to be ingenious, to think not in terms of the week, the month or the year, or even with the framework of a single war. In the First World War, the young men marched happily into enlistment lines and trenches, spurred by visions of heroism and dreams of glory, with none of this protest or antiwar nonsense. I saw that eventually history would offer such a moment to us again. We had to conceive a plan in terms of decades, generations. We had to prepare immediately for history's cycle to return.''

The general descended several more steps. ''I was willing to wait—twenty, thirty years, longer if it was necessary—to pass the torch to a younger, like-minded individual. I asked myself, how could we deliberately tap the natural human impulses for war, seize the imaginations of a new generation of young men at precisely the right moment?''

The general clenched his fist as if he had snatched the answer from midair and held it before him like a bony mace. He descended halfway down the stairs, his eyes fixed on Barrabas. His voice rang with passionate conviction.

''I looked to history for the answer, and I found it. Sixty years ago, when Germany was humiliated after the First World War. Their country disgraced, a whole new generation spurned their parents' dishonor and the shameful Weimar Republic that had grown from the ashes of German military defeat. The military machine they created swept across Europe.''

General Guetz signaled to the four men who watched from behind the glass wall of the boardroom. Wordlessly, the industrialist, the arms merchant, the movie mogul and the politician filtered from the boardroom and stood on the balcony, watching Barrabas, their faces expressionless.

''The solution to my dilemma became perfectly clear,'' General Guetz said calmly. ''If we must lose

Vietnam, it must be as humiliating a defeat as possible. So humiliating that America will'be ashamed, so shameful that a subsequent generation will feel disgraced. I called it the Weimar Syndrome.''

"That's why you betrayed your own country? Turning our military secrets over to the enemy?'' Barrabas shook his head in disbelief.

"How else do you think the North Vietnamese were able to pour down over South Vietnam, swarming like ants over the husk of that little country until they were beating at the gates of Saigon?'' Guetz roared angrily. "And you knew all along. How ironic, then, that you were also the last man out. I remember the photograph in all the newspapers, you leaping heroically from the roof of the American Embassy to grab the skid of the final departing helicopter. It's just the kind of thing that tantalizes the imaginations of young people today.''

Barrabas stared at the old retired general, whose face quivered with growing emotion, and he felt an immense sadness. His mind went back…the last helicopter lifting from the roof, the final realization that all those years of duty in Southeast Asia had been for naught. How could he explain the asphyxiating sense of loss to a new generation of young men: the wasted lives, his own, and those of the men and women who had been his friends and who now were dead.

On that hot Saigon day, the torment was over. He was alone on the highest roof of the beleaguered embassy. From below came the desperate roar of thousands who were being left behind. He stretched toward the skid of the helicopter hovering overhead, arms reached out to grab him, and he was lifted from a maelstrom spinning in an ocean of blood.

"The time has come, Colonel Barrabas," Guetz's voice rang from the stairs. "Sooner than my most fervent hopes. There is a new generation in America today who are ignorant of the battlefield. They lust for heroism, adventure, anything to remove them from their humdrum ordinary existences. They crave war, Colonel Barrabas! Humiliation is like money in the bank. It's time to draw on it."

The four men at the top of the stairs watched silently. A smile creased General Guetz's craggy face.

"It's a fact of life, Colonel. War is a part of human nature, and nature is not delicate. Which form of ruthlessness do you choose—flood or hurricane, plague or earthquake or volcanic eruption?"

"I got news for you, Guetz. America just isn't built that way. We believe in human dignity, that we're more than just animals gripped by savage impulses. War is an act of hatred, waged against the young by old men who are servants of death. Nature may be ruthless. It takes a human being to show compassion."

The general glanced at his Rolex. "We've spent enough time at this."

"Why did you go to Jessup? To deflect suspicion from yourself? Or to lure me into the open?"

"Perhaps it was just to see how you reacted." The general smiled. He turned to the gunmen on either side of the room. "Gentlemen, his time is up. Kill him in exactly thirty seconds. Colonel Barrabas, goodbye."

NATE BECK THREW HIMSELF back from the table, clutching the headphones. Through the windows on his left he saw the tiny shadow of the chopper through the drizzle. In one of the twin towers on his right, Barrabas was about to die.

The TOW missile waited at the window. The computer wizard ran to the optical sensor. The tube was locked in on the lower floor of the two-story office complex. He moved it slightly higher, to the concrete buttress between the two floors, and fired.

The plate glass window shattered outward like a sheet of ice, and the thin wire filaments streamed through the opening. The wire-guided missile fluttered like silk, and grew quickly smaller, closing the distance between itself and the skyscraper straight in its path.

THE SOLDIERS OF BARRABAS skimmed over a building, the helicopter still ascending toward the roof of the hundred-and-ten story World Trade Center when the TOW hit. Huge chunks of cement blasted into the sky and rained down. The building trembled and shivered from top to bottom. Shock waves rippled through the concrete and steel structure.

"Outa time!" Nanos yelled. "Let's just fly on by and shoot it out from up here!"

Liam O'Toole thrust his head into the cockpit.

"How steady can you fly this thing, say twenty, thirty feet offside the building?"

"Pretty steady." Bishop nodded, looking over his shoulder with a little smile. "Barring a little turbulence off the side of the building."

"Nothing like going in the new door," Nanos cracked.

O'Toole looked at him. "How's your broad jump, Alex?"

GUETZ'S HIRELINGS raised their weapons just as the building shuddered. The steel structure thundered, the floor cracked like river ice in breakup, and the outer walls disintegrated into a coarse powder. The jangling laughter of shattering glass was followed by cries and screams.

The politician and the movie mogul dropped from the balcony like torn sacks of potatoes and lay where they fell. Barrabas rolled between them, closer to the gaping edge of the building, and came up firing. The Browning spat its deadly kiss once, twice, and a gunman slapped against the wall, then the third time, and the second one went down before he could get up.

At the top of the stairs, the plump arms merchant teetered, covered in blood and impaled through the gut on a long cruel shard of plate glass. He was very much alive. Horror circling his eyes, he saw Barrabas and began stepping carefully down the stairs.

The mercenary fired twice. The Saudi's face disappeared behind a mask of blood. He tipped forward, driving the shard into the floor and shivering down its long length until his nose met the carpet.

The general was lying in a heap at the foot of the stairs. Barrabas ran to him, grabbing his collar. He flipped him over. Guetz opened his eyes, sputtering and insolent. Barrabas dragged him to his knees and jammed the Browning against his temple.

Suddenly the rhythmic clatter of a helicopter reverberated through the room. The LongRanger appeared from the grayness and floated just beyond the broken walls of the upper story.

IN THE HELICOPTER'S COCKPIT, Bishop sweated, his senses reaching through the flight controls into the metal and fiberglass structure to feel for the slightest pounding of turbulence that could wrench them away from the building. With minute movements, he made tiny adjustments to the collective and throttle, cyclic pitch and antitorque to counteract the constant change in the vortex of air batting against the aircraft.

Liam O'Toole opened the side window and rested a tube launcher on the rim. He squeezed the release, and grappling hooks soared into the skyscraper's open wound, carrying a cable across the forty-foot span. Lee secured the other end to a steel hook in the copter.

"You're not really going to do this, are you?" she asked the big Irish merc. He threw open the door and clipped his rappel harness to the cable. The helicopter floated rhythmically up and down. Outside, the cable fluttered and swung.

"It's my idea, ain't it."

"But I'm smaller, I'm lighter," Hatton insisted. "I can move faster."

Before O'Toole could reply, Nanos shouted from the cockpit. "It's the colonel! I see him! Inside the building!"

"ON YOUR FEET!" Barrabas ordered the general, shouting over the noise of the chopper and the scream of the wind.

The general's answer was wiped out by the tremendous racket, but he mouthed "where." His face was stricken by fear. He staggered against the gusts of wind and drizzle but rose to his feet, putting his arm out to hold on to Barrabas.

The merc pushed him away, pointing the pistol up the stairs. General Guetz leaned into the wind and started climbing. The barrel of the Browning prodded him on. The winding staircase clattered against the wall as they ascended to the top floor of the two-story office. The floor of the mezzanine had cracked and hung on a dangerous incline. A giant chunk of concrete was connected to the rest of the building by a few thin threads of steel rods. It swayed up and down like a tongue in the wind. The helicopter floated without apparent effort beyond. The street lay far away, fifty-five stories down.

Barrabas grabbed the general from behind, pulling him aside as the harpoon shot in front of them. It fell, its barbed hooks encircling the chunk of floor and an iron rod. It held tight. The silver cable sparkled across the void.

"What are you doing!" the general shouted into Barrabas's ears. The colonel looked at him. Somehow the general figured they were all going to get out of there together.

The door of the chopper opened, and the aircraft rose slightly. Liam O'Toole appeared at the door. He closed his eyes and let go. The alternative was death, but the ride itself was a thrill. He opened his eyes, and the boardroom of the Liberty Tribune was coming at him like the side of a doll house in the land of the small.

He swung inside the skyscraper, his feet running across the wavering chunk of floor, and stopped right in front of Barrabas.

"Guess again, Guetz!" Barrabas shouted at the traitor.

Guetz clutched Barrabas's sleeve. "What do you mean!" he screamed.

"Didn't know about your friend, sir!" O'Toole shouted. He held out a second harness. "I only brought one."

Barrabas took it. To O'Toole's astonishment, he handed it to the general. Guetz held it away from him like a dead rat.

"No time! I'll ride with you!" the mercenary shouted to the Irishman.

O'Toole nodded, turning back and giving the signal to the chopper. Bishop lowered it. The colonel wrapped his arms and legs around the ex-sergeant and held tight.

"No-o-o! You can't leave me!" Guetz ran forward, clawing at the colonel's back as the mercs swung away, streaming down the cable and into the side of the waiting helicopter. He looked at the harness. With a wrenching screech, the chunk of floor sank lower, pulling away from the building. It was held to the skyscraper only by several feet of iron rods. There was no way back. General Guetz jumped into the harness and snapped it together.

In the chopper, Bishop's hands were slippery with sweat. He lowered the bird, leaning into the building to shorten the span and give it a downward slant. Winds blowing up the side of the building pounded the fuselage. The blades stalled briefly when they ran out of air to deflect, and the engine screamed with the uneven velocity of the rotor. He was losing torque control, and the helicopter was beginning to swing from side to side.

Hatton and Nanos stood on either side of the open door, their arms stretched out to receive the two mercs. They popped in through the open side, and Lee unsnapped the harness from the cable.

"Did you leave someone behind?" she screamed over the deafening racket, pointing at the skyscraper. Guetz was visible in his boardroom, his hands working feverishly at the harness.

"I can't hold it!" Bishop shouted. A fistful of wind slammed into the belly of the chopper, knocking the mercs from their feet. They scrambled to hold on. The open door flapped and the chopper fishtailed, the torque wildly out of control.

Barrabas reached up and unclipped the cable.

The rotor stalled, and the chopper sank lower.

In the boardroom of the Liberty Tribune, the general clipped his cable to the harness and kicked away.

"Go!" Barrabas screamed at Bishop.

The pilot angled away from the skyscraper, doing autorotations until the engines caught and the rotor clipped again, pulling them higher. He circled toward the Hudson River.

General Guetz sailed gracefully to the end of the cable and pitched into space, plummeting in less than a minute to the plaza, fifty-four stories below. Barrabas leaned against the window, transfixed, until the twin towers and the falling body were enveloped by the distance and thickening fog.

"Tell Beck to get out fast!" Barrabas ordered. "Before this city goes berserk!"

The Greek turned from the copilot's seat. "He's on his way. The city is shrieking with sirens, and there are choppers heading in from all directions."

"Of the armed-police variety, no doubt," O'Toole added. "And they'll be after us soon. I wouldn't be feeling kindly toward returning to the heliport."

"The harbor's filled with fog, and Hayes is on his way to rendezvous there. We'll have to ditch the chopper."

"Yeah, all we have to do is find the Statue of Liberty in this weather," Bishop said dryly.

"Why did you go in by yourself, Colonel?" Lee Hatton demanded. "You know we would have gone there with you."

"Private matter," Barrabas remarked, heaving a sigh. He theatrically lifted his wounded leg with the blood-soaked bandage around the thigh. Lee gasped in shock, changing instantly from warrior to doctor. Barrabas smiled warmly at the mercs. "Besides, I took care of all the contingencies."

14

"Look at this, Nile," Walker Jessup said, lifting his head from the newspaper. "'Nuther shitload of trouble you guys kicked up again."

Barrabas grinned. "There weren't any witnesses, but there are so many stories floating around already that they'll never figure out what happened."

"And a lot of people are saying fine things about dear old General Guetz, a man supposedly loyal to his country."

"He's tainted, Jessup. He died a violent death. It's the one that got away that I wonder about."

"Was there?"

"There were four men there. In the end, I only saw three bodies. He'll be back. I have a feeling he's been around before." He pushed himself from the chair, leaning on his cane, and limped toward the door of Jessup's office. "I gotta do some things."

The rotund Fixer came around his desk, slipping a red velvet folder under his arm.

"Anna," he said, "She's neat."

Barrabas nodded. "Yup. Thanks for getting there. How did you handle the police?"

"When the real police got there, they encountered some Company personnel masquerading as detectives from the attorney general's and coroner's offices. The mess just disappeared, falling into the oblivion of overlapping jurisdictions.''

Jessup took the folder from under his arm and opened it up to the menu of La Guanillo. He closed in on the colonel, nudging him secretively with his elbow.

"Dinner's on me. Bermuda. Next Tuesday at eight. Bring a friend." He winked. "I made a fortune in the stock market, and I'm cashing it in!"

WELL, HELL, the mercenary thought, arriving at street level on his way out of the midtown building. Jessup made a show of not being concerned about anything beyond his stomach. Just like Barrabas made a show of being tough when it suited him.

He took a taxi to Grand Central Station, where Deke Howard waited in the slick rainy darkness. Howard climbed into the cab and looked at Barrabas, first with apprehension, then with relief.

"You're sure about this?"

"Sure I'm sure."

The taxi plunged into the wet November night. Soon they were on a bridge to Queens.

"Did Jessup tell you he might have work from time to time?"

The veteran nodded, visibly pleased. "I'm on the payroll this weekend. Some Saudi sheikh's kid wants to go to a disco. I wear a suit and dark glasses and look big and tough." Howard laughed. "But I think I'll stick to the small-time stuff, you know. Why did you do it for me, Colonel?"

"Almost fifteen years later we all come together again—you, me, Jessup and the general. Four men from the jungle."

"I remember," Deke said quietly, staring straight ahead. "It seemed like hours waiting in the marshes of the Kap Long River, Jessup pacing back and forth on the deck of the *Callisto*. He insisted that we wait the extra hour, then another half hour. The swamp had eyes, and every minute we sat there we were aware of them, invisible, watching, thinking. Oh, God, to be hunted. To be prey. It's awful.

"And then you came, stumbling through muck and over the bleached limbs of fallen trees to the patrol boat, where we pulled you in, happy that our wait and our fear had been worthwhile. You were beaten and bruised and bleeding, and your clothes were in rags, yet all you did was ask for Walker Jessup, salute and hand him the papers. But then I saw your eyes, and I remember thinking, this man has come back from hell."

"I remember when I was crawling on my belly through the swamps and jungle how thankful I was that the rainy season hadn't begun," Barrabas said. "It wasn't until I saw the *Callisto* that I remembered your concern about the low water levels. Still, for a while there it looked like we were going to make it. Then they hit us."

Howard took a deep breath. The memory that returned was a hard one. "You took that M-60 machine gun like it was a pistol and started mowing down everything along the bank."

The mercenary nodded absently. "You know, when I think about it, it's not as if I'm remembering. It's more like I'm watching myself do things. As if I was suspended over the boat, observing without feeling. I was on automatic pilot. I didn't think. We were fighting for our lives."

"Yeah. Doing a hell of a job, too. Until that 57 mm shell came out of nowhere and blew the bridge to smithereens. 'Course, I don't really remember that part, not after that piece of metal the size of a shoe box bashed in the back of my head. And they say a bullet peeled your helmet open like a can opener."

"Jessup got us out of there. He thought he was piloting a ship of dead men."

"The story was that the bullet came close to turning you into a permanent vegetable, and that was how your hair turned white. But that's not it, is it?"

Barrabas stared straight ahead for a few moments, knowing the difficulty with words, which always seemed to fail. He shook his head slightly, just enough to say no.

"The last thing I saw, when I was blasting at the shore with the M-60, was a face peering through the elephant grass on the left bank." He swallowed. "A face with blue eyes. There was only one man in that jungle with blue eyes, and he wasn't Vietcong."

Barrabas twisted uncomfortably in his seat. "I don't know what was worse, the death traps in the jungle, or seeing that traitor humiliate America like that. Cowards are despicable. You know what bothered me most about seeing Guetz hand over those secrets? He didn't bat an eye. Not even a twinge of remorse."

"Like a statue?" Deke asked. "I've got to learn to stop being like that. To feel again. If I don't, people like Guetz will have achieved at least part of their mad intentions."

"I hear you," said Barrabas. "And I think you're on your way."

Streetlights shone circles through the bare limbs of trees along the narrow boulevard. The taxi slowed before a small suburban house. Lights shone warmly in the windows.

"This is it," Deke said, reaching for the door handle. "I don't know what this will be like. Meeting my wife again. Her new husband. My son for the first time in ten years."

The front-porch light came on, and the inside door opened. A woman stood at the glass of the storm door, a young teenager beside her. She waved tentatively. The teenager stared, curious and shy.

"They wanted to see you."

"It'll take awhile I guess. For all of us."

"Yeah, but—" Barrabas pointed at Deke's son "—when you get to know him, tell him about it. He's the one you gotta look out for now. The new generation. Let's pray they don't make the mistakes we did."

Deke Howard climbed from the car. "What was the line from that song they used to sing back in the sixties? 'Teach your children well'?"

"Amen," Barrabas seconded.

Deke Howard closed the door, and the white-haired mercenary turned to the driver.

"Manhattan," he said. "Somewhere near Alphabet City."

HE TOOK THE STAIRS slowly with the cane and the stiff leg. Anna was waiting for him at her door. She let it fall open. When he came into the room, she backed away.

In a burst of anger, she threw herself at him, beating her fists against his chest.

"I know all about this, disappearing from a telephone call, and then men are coming into my house and then you come, and you leave me here alone."

Barrabas remained by the door, immobile, accepting her fury until she fell against him, exhausted, holding him and burying her face against his chest.

"It happened before in Poland." Her voice was a whisper. "I cannot take it again. That lover—" she shivered "—he is dead."

She looked up at Barrabas and read in his eyes his acknowledgement. She was right.

"I guess the hero doesn't always get the girl," Barrabas said slowly. He brushed against her, breathed in her scent, and with a finger wiped a tear from the corner of her eye. He put his arms around her.

Bravely smiling, she tried to laugh.

"But the gentleman always gets the lady." She reached around his neck and hugged him slowly. "At least, just one more time."

ERIC HELM

VIETNAM: GROUND ZERO

An elite jungle fighting group of strike-and-hide specialists fight a dirty war half a world away from home. This is more than action adventure. Every novel in this series is a piece of Vietnam history brought to life, from the Battle for Hill 875 to the Tet Offensive and the terror of the infamous Hanoi Hilton POW camp, told through the eyes of an American Special Forces squad. These books cut close to the bone, telling it the way it really was.

"Vietnam at Ground Zero is where this book is written. The author has been there, and he knows. I salute him and I recommend this book to my friends."

—Don Pendleton,
creator of The Executioner

Mack Bolan's

by Dick Stivers

Action writhes in the reader's own streets
as Able Team's Carl "Ironman" Lyons,
Pol Blancanales and Gadgets Schwarz
make triple trouble in blazing war. Join
Dick Stivers's Able Team as it returns to
the United States to become the country's
finest tactical neutralization squad in an
era of urban terror and unbridled crime.

"Able Team will go anywhere, do anything,
in order to complete their mission. Plenty
of action! Recommended!"
—*West Coast Review of Books*

Able Team titles are available
wherever paperbacks are sold.

AT-1

TAKE 'EM NOW

FOLDING SUNGLASSES
FROM GOLD EAGLE

Mean up your act with these tough, street-smart shades. Practical, too, because they fold 3 times into a handy, zip-up polyurethane pouch that fits neatly into your pocket. Rugged metal frame. Scratch-resistant acrylic lenses. Best of all, they can be yours for only $6.99.

MAIL YOUR ORDER TODAY.

Send your name, address, and zip code, along with a check or money order for just $6.99 + .75¢ for postage and handling (for a total of $7.74) payable to Gold Eagle Reader Service. (New York and Iowa residents please add applicable sales tax.)

Remove from pouch...

unfold once...

unfold twice...

and they're ready to wear.

GOLD EAGLE

Gold Eagle Reader Service
901 Fuhrmann Blvd.
P.O. Box 1396
Buffalo, N.Y. 14240-1396

GES-1A

Offer not available in Canada.